"I thought you were dead,
remember? How would I know
you had a...daughter?"

Alec didn't sound angry, but he looked as
though he were poised to strike or waiting for a
blow to fall.

Somewhat angrily, Cait realized he didn't even
so much as suspect the truth. She tried pulling
away from him, but he didn't let her go. He
held her while his daughter continued crying
for attention.

"How old is your baby, Cait?" he asked.

In her fantasies, in the dreams in which Alec
hadn't been taken away from her, he had
known every detail of their daughter's life.
Now he didn't even know her age.

Alec didn't repeat his question. Cait's pale
face, her quivering lips, even the odd apology
in her eyes, told him more clearly than any
words that the baby upstairs was his.

A little girl. A daughter.

His child.

Dear Reader,

The weather may be cooling off as fall approaches, but the reading's as hot as ever here at Silhouette Intimate Moments. And for our lead title this month I'm proud to present the first longer book from reader favorite BJ James. In *Broken Spurs* she's created a hero and heroine sure to live in your mind long after you've turned the last page.

Karen Leabo returns with *Midnight Confessions*, about a bounty hunter whose reward—love—turns out to be far different from what he'd expected. In *Bringing Benjy Home*, Kylie Brant matches a skeptical man with an intuitive woman, then sets them on the trail of a missing child. *Code Name: Daddy* is the newest Intimate Moments novel from Marilyn Tracy, who took a break to write for our Shadows line. It's a unique spin on the ever-popular "secret baby" plotline. And you won't want to miss *Michael's House*, Pat Warren's newest book for the line and part of her REUNION miniseries, which continues in Special Edition. Finally, in *Temporary Family* Sally Tyler Hayes creates the family of the title, then has you wishing as hard as they do to make the arrangement permanent.

Enjoy them all—and don't forget to come back next month for more of the best romance fiction around, right here in Silhouette Intimate Moments.

Leslie Wainger,
Senior Editor and Editorial Coordinator

Please address questions and book requests to:
Silhouette Reader Service
U.S.: 3010 Walden Ave., P.O. Box 1325, Buffalo, NY 14269
Canadian: P.O. Box 609, Fort Erie, Ont. L2A 5X3

CODE NAME: DADDY

MARILYN TRACY

Silhouette®
INTIMATE™MOMENTS®

Published by Silhouette Books

America's Publisher of Contemporary Romance

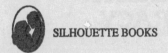 SILHOUETTE BOOKS

ISBN 0-373-07736-X

CODE NAME: DADDY

Printed in U.S.A.

MARILYN TRACY

lives in Portales, New Mexico, in a ramshackle turn-of-the-century house with her son, two dogs, three cats and a poltergeist. Between remodeling the house to its original Victorian-cum-Deco state, writing full-time and finishing a forty-foot cement dragon in the backyard, Marilyn composes full soundtracks to go with each of her novels.

After having lived in both Tel Aviv and Moscow in conjunction with work for the U.S. State Department, Marilyn enjoys writing about the cultures she's explored and the people she's grown to love. She likes to hear from people who enjoy her books and always has a pot of coffee on or a glass of wine ready for anyone dropping by, especially if they don't mind chaos and know how to wield a paintbrush.

To my wonderful family

Prologue

Caitlin Leigh. I will remember you all the seconds of my life.

Locked in each other's arms, in a windowless prison, cushioned only by their own clothing and a mildewed, paint-splattered drop cloth, Alec couldn't see Cait's eyes. He could have reached up and pulled the cord that would flood them in harsh fluorescent light, but much as he craved seeing her eyes, he needed to hold her close against him even more.

"I told you my middle name," Cait said. "What's yours?"

"Hmm?"

"You're not going to tell me, are you?"

"Doesn't look like it."

He savored the way her body vibrated as she chuckled against him. He felt he'd squandered the first twenty-four hours with her, letting the precious minutes slip away, unnoticed, not realizing in the course of that first day what she would come to mean to him.

He didn't know if it was night or day and strangely, with Cait tucked against him, he found separation of time no longer mattered. They'd been granted sporadic meals and even more infrequent nature reliefs. The hours stretched into an infinity made all the more sharply clarified by the simple awareness that everything would end soon.

Alec knew Cait was as aware of their imminent deaths as he, though she hadn't talked about it after that first long day together. He forced himself to breathe naturally so as not to frighten her now. But Alec couldn't stop thinking about the stark fact that the terrorists holding them prisoner had marked Cait for death if their demands weren't met within three days.

Three days had surely passed in the time he and Cait had been locked together. Any minute that closet door could open and they would take Cait from him and execute her.

And Alec, perhaps better than anyone, knew the terrorists' demands would never be met.

Alec unconsciously tightened his arms around Cait's slender, lovely body, as if holding her closer he could somehow pull her inside himself, protecting her, saving her. But in his heart he knew, maybe for the first time in his life, he was nearly powerless.

Strangely, with Cait nestled against him, he didn't suffer true despair; the time for that bleak emotion lay in the not-so-distant future. That they were going to die was a certainty, that he had precious moments left with Cait was an unexpected gift.

He traced her jawline with his thumb, and higher, along her cheek. She was an incredible woman, he thought. Slated for death in a matter of minutes or hours, imprisoned in a filthy utility closet with a complete stranger, she'd somehow stayed sane and saucy. She'd valiantly matched his humor, outstripped his denial, and joined his need to expunge thoughts of death by turning to incredible passion instead.

He hadn't told her he'd been in countless dangerous situations before; there would have been no point beyond recounting his exploits. Besides, he'd never been involved in anything as dire as this particular crisis. Because until this particular crisis, his heart had never been lying on his vulnerable shoulder.

Holding Cait tightly against him, he wanted to tell her who, what he was. But telling her now would be like admitting defeat. Somehow, even in recognizing their inevitable death, Cait had still managed to cling to a modicum of hope, and confessing his background, his training, would be tantamount to dousing even that small flicker of possibility.

When had the passion that flared between them metamorphosed into tenderness? Was it sometime during a quiet exchange of childhood memories? That good old black Lab-cross he'd had as a kid. Cait's beloved Aunt Margaret's antics with her motley collection of shelter-adopted animals—seven at last count. The pain Cait suffered at the loss of her parents, a loss he understood from the dark days when his brother died. Had it been during the swapping of favorite music, books and movies? Or had the tenderness come afterward, when fires ebbed and Cait first curled into his bare body, trust relaxing all muscles but those waiting for their prison door to open?

God knew, he'd tried every trick and ploy in the book to escape, but the terrorists holding them were pros and had foiled each attempt almost before he executed it. But Alec suspected the real reason he hadn't gone for an all-out final play was Cait; he couldn't jeopardize whatever slim chance she had for survival. If by some miracle negotiations were successful, Cait should be alive to enjoy her release and she wouldn't be if he attempted utility-closet heroics. And if negotiations failed, he had to be around still to use his trump card: his life for hers.

Alec cursed a dark-humored, unsympathetic fate. That he should meet Cait here, now, wasn't fair. He supposed that somewhere in the back of his mind he'd always known that one distant day his number would come up, that he wouldn't be able to use brain and brawn to duck a bullet or dodge a knife.

He was uncomfortably aware that Cait would never have thought such a thing. She was young, pretty, a software designer whose conversation skipped from sharp logic to the delightfully absurd. Computer hackers weren't generally earmarked for early death at the hands of killers.

He opened his mouth to tell her some of this, any of his thoughts, any of his chaotic plans, even his middle name, but stopped when she pressed a kiss into his palm, calling him back to this rare moment of peace. He had to close his eyes against a strange pain deep inside him.

He stroked her face aware of a profound gratitude.

Could he possibly be insane enough to feel grateful to the terrorists? It was a common enough hostage response, he knew from his many years of training and experience. But his wasn't the classic thank-you-for-stopping-beating-me syndrome, but a heartfelt awareness that if the terrorists hadn't thrown Cait and he together, he would never have known her at all.

How very much he would have missed. He pressed his lips against her forehead and stayed there. If he had his way, he would stay there forever.

"If you could live in any house, anywhere, what kind of house would it be?" she asked, her voice muffled against his chest. Her fingers slowly traced a scar from a bullet that found him years before, as if she knew he'd come close to death from that one also, but in their time together she hadn't asked about it.

What kind of house? *A kind with you in it,* he thought, and smiled. She'd asked many such whimsical questions in the past couple of days. In their short time together, she'd taught him to follow her flights of fancy, to visualize her dreams and, finally, as a means of mental escape, to create them himself.

"I'd live in the country," he said. She murmured in satisfaction. With a lover's eye as contractor, he built a fine, old farmhouse Cait might like. "The house would stand back from the road, hidden in a stand of tall trees."

"Oaks and maples."

"Yes. Trees that change to reds and golds in the fall." His smile broadened. He could see it.

"Two stories?"

"Absolutely. With a funny little attic you have to bend over in."

She chuckled and this time the feel of her laughter against his bare chest almost broke his heart. "The attic would have little windows in the eaves. And lots of nooks and crannies. A place where kids can go and pretend they're pirates."

"Or kings," she said.

"Or astronauts."

In this darkness, death waiting for them at any moment, the attic in his make-believe house seemed more real than any place he'd ever been.

"Tell me about the kitchen," she said, luring him downstairs with her rich contralto voice. "I already know it's warm."

And he saw it, too, could smell the clean pine scent of the polished floor planks, the garlic and fresh parsley hanging from pegs above the countertops. "It's big, the kind you can cook in while a whole party of people crowd in to help. Pans hang from a circular ring above a butcher-block island. One wall—"

"Has a great fireplace."

"With a mantel."

"For pictures of the kids."

"For pictures of the kids," he repeated, his heart performing a slow flip as he could see school pictures tucked in an odd assortment of antique frames collected from garage sales and auctions. A little boy—blond like Cait, a little girl, dark like him.

"Is there a window? I see a window somewhere," Cait said. Her voice was tremulous now, and the hand on his shoulder gripped with almost painful intensity.

He had to clear his throat to speak. "Better than that. There are French doors on the left side, and through them you can see the back lawn."

"It's lush and green."

"And bright with rain from an afternoon shower."

"And outside is a picnic table."

"Beneath one of the huge oak trees." He could see the preparations for the picnic already out on the kitchen's butcher-block table, a checkered cloth, a basket filled with goodies, a treasure trove of promise.

"And after the kids go to bed, we'll go through those French doors, drink cheap wine and make a wish on the first star."

She kissed him then, almost fiercely, as if sealing a pledge. He responded equally fervently, not from desire this time, but as if by kissing her now he could make the pretty illusion become reality somewhere, somehow.

They'd found something rare and remarkable, an ability to transcend terror by touch, by words, and finally, in this strange prison, by weaving a dream so beautiful and so rich a kiss could make it happen.

They dressed slowly, not talking, Alec half afraid that any acknowledgment of the present would make it come crashing in on them. In the light now, seeing Cait's mussed blond hair, the shadows beneath her green eyes, Alec wished he could really make her promises, ached to assure her that all would be well, that a future did wait for her, for them.

Alec had to clear his throat before he could speak. "My middle name—"

The door of their prison exploded inward and Alec instinctively jerked Cait behind him, trying with a last-second desperation to block her from harm. One of the four terrorists, probably a second in command, jabbed at him with the point of his deadly 9 mm semiautomatic.

Alec could see by the look in the men's faces that something had changed. Something had gone wrong with their plans. They no longer looked merely dangerous, they were murderous in their frantic need for action, wild-eyed in their loss of control.

He felt a hopelessness steal over him, but still he kept Cait behind him. "You don't need her," he said. "Take me."

"The woman," the man with the assault rifle said, making another jab at Alec.

"You don't get it, pal," Alec said. "I'm FBI—"

Even as Alec was spitting out his words, the terrorist was flipping the rifle around. He gave a vicious swipe to Alec's head, hitting him exactly where Vandever himself had performed the same trick two days before. The blow wiped any explanations away. The room exploded into neon colors then tilted sharply. Despite every desire warring with gravity, Alec crumpled and slumped to the side.

Through a haze of pain Alec heard Cait cry out as he fell back against the wall of their prison and slid to the drop cloth they'd abandoned on the floor. One of the terrorists grabbed Cait by the hair and arm, dragging her from the closet. The other, the one who had struck him, lifted his gun and pointed it at Alec.

Cait's scream pierced the murk and Alec blinked away the mist, staring into the barrel of the rifle while taking in Cait's pain-racked form. Cait called his name, her voice echoing in the small room, and then the sound was drowned out by the sharp reports of the semiautomatic. Alec felt the hot impacts and saw Cait convulse as if the bullets had struck her instead. She screamed again and fought her captor. Her head was cruelly wrenched back and she was dragged from the doorway.

Alone in the closet, a dark burning in his chest, Alec knew he was dying. He tried lifting a hand to his wounds and even this small effort seemed monumental. He could feel blood seeping from his body and could smell the sharp scent of copper, could taste it in his mouth.

Somewhere down the corridor, out of sight, Cait continued to scream.

And after the kids go to bed . . .

He felt his body growing cold and the world growing indistinct. He wanted to close his eyes and let the cold take him, but Cait's screams lashed him awake. He had to tell her something, but couldn't remember what it was.

We'll go through those French doors...

Then, surrounding Cait's screams, Alec heard other shouting, other voices. Maybe they could help him remember what it was he needed to tell her. Something about his name.

We'll drink cheap wine...

And then...two gunshots, one after another. Muffled. The sound a weapon makes at point-blank contact. And Cait's screams ceased.

And make a wish on the first star.

But there were no more stars. Cait was gone.

Alec closed his eyes and let the cold take him.

Chapter 1

Friday, November 9, 5:50 p.m. MST
Two years later

Alec pulled his glasses from his face and rubbed the bridge of his nose. His back ached with a grinding, brutal demand for surcease. His neck was stiff and made him long for soft hands that could knead away tension.

He wanted to growl, wanted to pound something, anything. But anger didn't help the pain in his body any more than it assuaged the torment in his mind. He shifted slightly, grimacing at the ripples of agony that sitting too long in one position inevitably produced. The misery that chewed on each individual muscle fiber in his chest and shoulders was a result of the shooting two years before, a pain endurable only because it was the least consequence of that particular day's horrors.

Alone, on an undercover assignment high in the New Mexico Rockies, he only talked face-to-face with the few Pecos villagers who sold food or gasoline. He'd grown a beard that gradually hid his features until the sheer size of it masked his identity completely, even if it couldn't hide the bleakness his mirror revealed in his eyes. He exercised daily, forcing his body to levels of endurance that had left him shaking and swearing for the first year and now only served to mitigate his anger.

And in the evenings he sat behind his computer, his unauthorized and wholly personal quest for vengeance magnified by the sheer weight of his enforced loneliness, intensified by his careful, methodical and ruthless need for an answer to a question he'd only just begun to understand.

Forswearing sleep, ignoring all but the basic need for food and water, he endlessly, restlessly searched his cache of compiled and stolen information, combing through each notation and photograph for the clue that would give him the one name behind the terrorists who had gunned him down and murdered Cait Wilson.

He glanced at his wristwatch and, seeing it was close to six o'clock, moved into the living room to catch the evening news. His cabin may have looked empty and his lifestyle might have felt woefully incomplete, but he managed the solitude by constant contact with the world outside the canyon. A computer, a telephone, a satellite dish, a coffeemaker and a television—and he was golden.

Alec clicked on the television set and sat down on his Salvation Army sofa, his elbows resting on his upraised knees. He pressed the remote until he found one of the primary networks. He stared at the screen, without consciously seeing the wrap-up of a talk show.

His thoughts kept swerving back to a memo he'd found just last week. As the tongue will probe a sore tooth, his mind kept prodding at the implications found in that damning document. And each nudge, each glancing touch raised more questions, greater confusion, and strengthened an already glassy, core-deep fury.

In some possibly misguided attempt to stay privy to the goings-on of his former division within the Federal Bureau of Investigation, he'd routinely culled all inter-office communication. He'd made his usual hit-and-run theft, downloading everything, and a password-encoded file had shown up in his private collection of misappropriated information. The urge for knowledge hadn't proved so misguided after all.

Two days of decoding finally produced an FBI memorandum of record, a detailed, lengthy memo outlining a top-secret internal investigation of a suspected, highly intricate cover-up of the soured hostage situation that took place two years ago at the World Health Organization in Washington, D.C.

The evening news opening credits rolled to unlikely jazz music but all Alec heard was the steady buzz of his own thoughts. For two years he'd assumed his role was the only lie to come out of that disaster. Unconscious and near death, he hadn't been in any shape to argue when the FBI announced to the world—and most of the FBI, as well—that agent Alec MacLaine had perished in the melee of gunfire that fateful morning in Washington. And to be honest, later he simply hadn't given a damn. Without Cait, knowing he hadn't been able to save her, he'd faced his ''death'' with a stoic and bitter acceptance. He'd even watched news clips of his so-called funeral, the full honors for a federal agent routine.

But the memo decoded during the past week revealed things said and done that Alec had never guessed. Apparently drafted by the new director of his former division, the memorandum questioned motives, rationales and statements issued by the FBI team taking the WHO that fateful morning. Most of the so-called "facts," claimed the memo, were in direct conflict with Alec MacLaine's deposition, and, as MacLaine had been in a coma at the inception of the cover-up, his testimony could be taken at face value.

After highlighting the list of stories slated for the evening, the station broke away for another commercial. Alec swore, but not because of the delay in hearing the news. He swore because he couldn't hit something, couldn't vent the rage boiling inside him as he mentally reviewed other points contained in the memo. The document suggested that the terrorists hadn't been random, that they hadn't been simply crazy zealots out for a day's suicidal madness. The author of the memo speculated that the terrorists had been after *him*. Period. End of story. Meaning Cait Wilson had been murdered just because she'd been in the wrong place at the worst of wrong times.

The understanding of this truth gnawed at Alec like so much broken glass. It had been bad enough just to know she no longer lived in this world, but to know that she'd died because of *him* was nearly unbearable.

But his very soul cringed at the next hideous and utterly paralyzing conjecture revealed in the memorandum. The author theorized that someone within Alec MacLaine's own division had put the contract out on him, had hired the killers and had orchestrated the cover-up.

In addition, the memorandum revealed a precise and remarkably current assessment of Alec's whereabouts, his assignment and his habits. The author implied the assignment was a make-work project only and that, until the investigation was completed, he was being kept out of sight and, therefore, out of danger.

Now, miles away from Washington, listening to a toothpaste commercial, he held information in his hands that could bring the entire FBI to its knees. He'd worked for the FBI for some fifteen years and never questioned the innate integrity of the organization. Now he did, and the realization sickened him.

Someone, someone he *knew,* had wanted him dead and had killed Cait in his place. If what the memo outlined was true, and he knew in the pit of his stomach that each word reeked of the rotten truth, then whichever of his former pals had orchestrated the setup two years ago had conceived of an utterly Machiavellian plan.

It would have been so very easy to take him out at any time; an assassin could practically be hired just by riffling through the classified section of any major newspaper. But this someone had used Alec's own business, his training and his expertise to kill him. This someone had neatly arranged for Alec MacLaine to perish at the very hands of the type of terrorist he'd been investigating.

The trouble was, he hadn't died. The question then became *Why not?* If the unnamed someone had created such an elaborate plan, why hadn't the terrorists just done as they were hired to do? What stopped them? Did they get greedy and want more money, guns, whatever? Besides which, if this someone had wanted him dead badly enough to arrange all the circus trappings, why hadn't that person just finished him off while he was in the hospital? So, the source of the hit hadn't necessarily cared if he lived or died so long as he was effectively out of the picture. And investigating a land-grant scheme in the mountains above Pecos, New Mexico, was about as out of the way as a man could get.

A pretty announcer introduced the evening news team and launched into the night's account of world trauma while Alec wondered which of his colleagues, his so-called *friends,* was going to find himself damned sorry Alec MacLaine hadn't really died two years ago.

The top story of the day was a live report from the scene of a hostage situation in one of New York City's convention centers.

Instantly Alec focused on the screen.

"To recap the events of the day, this morning shortly after opening ceremonies at a convention of left-wing activists, four masked and heavily armed gunmen broke into the convention hall, barricaded the doors and took some fifty conferees hostage. Police report that at present none of the hostages have been released and, as far as they can ascertain, none killed, though the terrorists are threatening loss of life if their demands are not met."

A muscle in Alec's jaw jerked as he clamped his teeth together. He stared at the screen but didn't see the mammoth convention center in the heart of the Big Apple. Instead, he saw the broad, curved, creamy interior of the World Health Organization in Washington, D.C.

As though from behind a news camera, he saw the man he'd been only two years ago, and watched that Alec MacLaine openly appreciating the pretty woman crossing the empty lobby. He was in the building that early in the morning, somewhere between dark and dawn, because he had a meeting with a source, a man who had promised to fill him in on a few details of the Aryan Nation's underground activities. The pretty woman had looked up at him, smiled and said, "Cold out, isn't it?"

Looking back, it was hard to imagine that he hadn't known she would become the single most important person in his life. He should have recognized her right then and there. Her smile, her throaty voice and her innocuous words.

"We have the NYPD police commissioner, Allen Jamison, with us tonight. Commissioner, exactly what demands are the terrorists making?"

The usual, Alec thought: transportation, money and the release of fellow psychotics. Different cause, same scenario, same bloody and horrible conclusion.

"And what can you tell us about the possibility of safely getting to the hostages?"

Next to none, Alec thought bitterly, though back then, as one of the two hostages, he'd certainly been praying somebody was trying their damnedest.

"Reaching the hostages isn't our first priority. The safety of those people being held inside has to remain our foremost concern. Getting to them may prove the most damaging. If you'll recall the hostage situation in Washington two years ago..."

Alec winced, recalling it in minute detail. One moment he'd been chatting with the pretty woman, making her smile, thinking how a lovely woman's smile was sometimes better than a month of straight sunshine, the next he'd been pinned against cool marbled walls, the barrel of a 9 mm assault rifle—the kind favored by Aryan Nation activists and White Separatists—brutally pressed against his jugular vein.

And the pretty woman—he hadn't even known her name then—was roughly pinned in another thug's arms, a deadly .357 Magnum distorting her full lips to a terrible grimace.

Their attackers didn't ask questions or make demands. They simply strong-armed their hostages into a janitorial closet and slammed and locked the door behind them. But Alec had seen enough to know the four men were professionals. He'd had the terrible suspicion the men were after him—it was only logical to assume he'd been set up, that the meeting was a ruse. But he'd never been sure and had been told point-blank during his days in the hospital that it wasn't true, that he'd only had the misfortune to be in the wrong place at the wrong time. Like Cait.

He should have known better. He should have trusted his instincts. He'd have been two years closer to avenging Cait's untimely death. Two years closer to taking down the man who had robbed the world of Cait's smile.

"And with their current demands, what do you feel is the likelihood of all hostages surviving this siege?"

"Nil," Alec said aloud. "They'll murder some innocent. Or many innocents. Then the bastards holding the guns will be killed."

As they had been two years ago. And dead men don't tell tales.

"And we don't want to risk the lives of any of our peace officers, either," the commissioner said.

"As happened in the WHO incident," the reporter added, briefly capsulizing the fall of federal agent Alec MacLaine.

That same fallen agent stared at the screen with dull bitterness. The doctors in the hospital had repeatedly told Alec he was lucky to be alive. But he hadn't felt lucky— he'd felt battered, chewed up and horribly cheated.

Then, slowly, he'd found a pain-deflection technique that compelled him to ignore the searing in his chest and shoulders, that drove him beyond the limits of endurance: revenge. It served as anodyne to his multiple wounds, painkiller for his tortured thoughts, and as an impetus to keep searching, keep tracking until he nailed the source responsible for ordering the terrorists into the WHO that tragic morning two years ago.

And now he knew his own paycheck came from that same organization. Damn them. Damn them all.

He wanted to kick at the television in a violent act of denial. But he didn't move, didn't duck the truth, even though everything in him rebelled against facing it. Hearing about this other hostage situation, remembering the past, continually replaying the memo, he knew with bile-black emotion that one of his *friends* had killed Cait Wilson. Murdered her as surely as if he'd pulled the trigger himself.

From the details in the memorandum, the primary suspect could be one of only three men. He could rule out most of the some seventeen agents in his division, simply by eliminating any cross-reference between his assignments and theirs. Anything remotely related to the Aryan Nation investigation he kept, and the list dropped to three with access, sufficient seniority and similar assignment schedules: Jack King, Fred Masters and Jorge Sifuentes.

All three he'd considered friends. They were men he'd eaten dinner with, shared the rare bottle of debriefing Scotch with, men whose children he could name, men he *knew*.

He'd entered the agency with Jack King, fourteen years before. They'd been in the same class, gone through the same exercises, retreats and psych examinations. They'd partnered for several missions, including the one that created the scar Cait had traced after making love two years before. Jack had a similar scar on his right flank, a reminder of a time he ate a bullet for Alec.

They'd swapped a thousand conspiracy theories and had collared more than their share of psychos and bad guys. They'd even run the occasional kitten-in-the-tree missions, the do-good public relations runs. Alec had held Jack's son at his christening, accepting the honor of godfather, and stood by Jack when his marriage failed and his family moved to California.

And Jack had fought right beside him every day of the grueling physical therapy, refusing to let him give up and accept a broken body. A man couldn't lay claim to a better friend than Jack. Or so he'd always believed.

Until now.

Fred Masters was also a good man in a tight spot. He'd covered Alec's tail more than once and was a veritable wizard at ferreting out vital information from the most unlikely sources. The polished Princeton man, with a degree in engineering as well as law, was an experienced agent when the ink hadn't dried on Jack's and Alec's fresh law degrees. When they opted for the bureau instead of hanging up a shingle, Fred had shown them many of the proverbial tricks of the trade, carefully grooming them to ascend the hierarchy of government service. Before the soured hostage situation, Alec had been a frequent visitor in the Masters's sprawling Virginia home.

He hadn't been there in two years now.

And Jorge Sifuentes was the brilliant up-and-comer. He could speak any of five different languages with more facility than most Americans tackled English. With his dark hair and flashing eyes, his only real problem was the constant entourage of beautiful women following him everywhere he went. His ready sense of the ridiculous was always close to the surface; he'd been the only one who had been able to bring a smile to Alec's lips in the past two years.

But facts didn't care about relationships, and to assume that one of these three men couldn't be corrupted, couldn't slide into that zone existing between honor and bankruptcy, or to cling to a belief that one of these fine men couldn't have taken that dangerous turn on the double-agent highway was tantamount to condoning their actions.

And he didn't, *couldn't,* let this cover-up lie. Not and live with himself. A woman had died. Cait had lost her life because of it.

Which one of his friends had killed Cait?

The on-the-scene reporter thanked the NYPD commissioner and sent Americans back to the studio announcer, who recapitulated everything discussed in the past few minutes. She told the viewing audience the studio was lucky today to have with them a guest from the Crisis Intervention Unit in Bethesda, Maryland, a survivor of the hostage incident in Washington two years before.

Alec felt as if someone had thrown a pitcher of ice water at his face. One of the survivors? There were none. Not even—according to the general public—him. His heart started to pound in heavy, thundering beats.

The television camera view shifted to a close-up of the survivor.

Alec's mouth went dry as he stared at the face of a dead woman.

Chapter 2

Friday, November 9, 6:15 p.m. MST

Alec closed his eyes, sure he was hallucinating, fantasizing again. He whipped them open, riveted to the screen. Her lovely face was still in front of him.

Cait!

It had to be some bizarre coincidence. Same features, same general type of work. But it was, had to be, a different woman; he'd heard the shots that killed her.

"Cait Wilson, designer of a software package crisis experts are hailing as the greatest boon to rescue workers since the portable gurney. Thank you for joining us at such short notice, Cait."

Same face... *same woman.* Cait was alive.

On-screen, Cait nodded and smiled slightly. She was calm, her features composed. She gave the impression of expertise, a deep inner peace, and yet something sad lingered in her eyes. When he'd seen her last, she'd been screaming, straining to break free of her captors.

"What we've done," Cait explained in that contralto voice that still had the capacity to make him shiver, "is to compile profuse amounts of psychological data collected from victims and survivors of emergency situations and constructed that data in such a way that rescue workers can simply call up a given situation—let's say an earthquake, for example—and cross-reference it with known factors, such as twelve-story building, built in the sixties, lots of glass windows, and so on. After all the physical parameters are established, we factor in the number of possible victims or survivors inside."

Her sandy blond hair was shorter than it had been two years ago, more businesslike. Then, it had been long enough that one of the terrorists had grabbed a handful of it, cruelly dragging her head back.

This night, before the news cameras, Cait's green eyes were clear and reflected the lights in whatever studio or office the reporter interviewed her. Then, tears of pain and anguish had flooded her eyes, drowning them. Drowning him.

"We've programmed in a wide variety of psychological responses based on crisis situations, such as how a mother with her children will react as opposed to a mother whose children are safe at home."

Cait disappeared as a facsimile of her program flashed across the screen and her voice continued to explain her software. Computer-imaged people ran for narrow doorways, jamming them, then falling as smoke or debris caught them. Other images showed rescue workers climbing through broken windows, rescue dogs reaching small children, and panicked employees ignoring fellow workers as they sought any means of escape.

Alec knew how they felt; his thoughts kept gumming up in the doorways of his mind.

"I understand rescue workers are using your program today to see what might be done for the hostages here in New York. Can you tell us a little bit of what that entails?"

Alec didn't hear Cait's response, he only listened to the cadence of her low-pitched voice, her lilting rhythm. It played on him like a musical instrument.

"You survived just such a traumatic incident two years ago in Washington, didn't you, Cait?"

No, Alec thought. Cait hadn't survived; she'd been murdered. The terrorists took her away and executed her. He *knew* this, had *known* it for two agonizing years. His hands were shaking, and his heartbeat was erratic.

"What in the hell—?" he whispered.

"You were one of the hostages the White Separatists held for three days," the interviewer stated.

Alec realized with a dim shock that he'd always thought in terms of murdered victims: Cait and himself. Dead but not.

As he frowned at the television, he saw that Cait no longer appeared calm. Her gaminlike features stilled, her eyes slightly flattened, as if she were poised for a hit. The question, for some reason, had upset her. God, how could he still know what would trouble her?

She hesitated, then said, "Yes." She looked down at her hands, then back at the camera. "Hopefully the software program I was showing you earlier will be able to help people in similar situations."

"The other hostage, a federal agent, and all four of the terrorists were killed when authorities rushed the building. How did it come about that you were the only survivor?" the interviewer asked, leaning forward. The question seemed to imply that Cait was guilty of wrong-doing.

Alec sat as if carved from stone. The interviewer had it wrong; he wasn't killed—even supposedly—when the FBI rushed the building. He suddenly realized how much the memorandum, so filled with truths, had still left unsaid. From the look on Cait's face and from the interviewer's words, Alec realized a very real possibility existed that the FBI had deliberately and cold-bloodedly mowed down the very terrorists someone within the FBI had hired. Dead men really don't tell tales.

"How did you manage to survive the gunfire, Cait?"

Alec leaned forward. Yes, *how?*

"I—I was just lucky, I guess," Cait stammered. She looked disconcerted by the question, uncertain of her standing.

Alec's heart thundered. How could she be alive?

"I understand this is the first interview you've granted since that morning two years ago," the interviewer said, her eyes as avid as a hungry wolf's.

"That's true," Cait said softly.

"Could you tell us why?"

Cait smiled and a slight glimmer of mischief lit her green eyes. "I wanted to publicize my new software package. As you can see, it offers—"

The interviewer interrupted Cait. "But are we correct in assuming you were closeted with slain federal agent Alec MacLaine for three days before his death?"

Cait's full lips tightened for a moment, and even from where he sat, a full fifteen hundred miles away, Alec knew the question—or interruption—had angered her. Her anger had been one of the things he most trusted in Cait. In the three days he'd known her, her ire was always accurate, always sincere and incredibly on target.

"Can you tell us something about him? Did he attempt to defuse the situation?"

"Of course he *tried*," Cait said impatiently, and added, "Alec MacLaine died trying to save my life." Then, very coldly, she added, "It was thanks to him that I got through it sane, let alone alive."

As if he were back there, as he'd been so many times in the past two years, Alec remembered the strong odor of ammonia, the mildewed drop cloth they'd used as a blanket, the roll of toilet paper Cait had used to wipe the blood from his forehead where one of the terrorists had smashed the gun butt before throwing them into the dark closet.

Alec rose to his feet. He mouthed her name, but couldn't force the necessary air through his lungs to gain control of his voice.

Unlike now, his legs hadn't been able to support him those first few hours in that narrow closet. Cait had held him, a total stranger, as if they'd known each other for years, as if it were only natural to meet a bleeding man in a utility closet while waiting for death. She'd held him, cradled him, muttering caustic word pictures of what would happen to the terrorists in the afterlife. Sometime during that enchanting, falsely brave monologue, his head had ceased swimming, and he'd managed a few suggestions himself. Her green eyes had met his with an odd combination of anger and humor, with only a latent acknowledgment of their inevitable death. He'd thought then, and nothing had changed his mind since, she was the most courageous woman he'd ever met.

Alec reached one unfeeling hand to the screen as if he could really touch her face again. In his mind he could feel the soft, warm curves of her lovely face, he remembered the velvet texture of her throat, the silk of her hair, the tears that spilled free more than once, tears that stained his heart forever and lingered even now on his tongue.

Alive. Not dead. *Alive and well.*

He heard her correcting the announcer's statement that Cait had worked in the World Health Organization. He remembered the reason she'd been there as vividly as he recalled every second of the time they'd spent together. She'd only dropped in to personally deliver a software package she could have sent later in the day by a bicycle courier. She had walked from her office on Fourth Street and had arrived at the WHO at the worst of all worst moments, just in time to be roughly seized along with the man they were really after.

If she hadn't chosen that morning to walk off her annoyance at a minor traffic accident, if she hadn't finished her software package on worldwide tracking of communicable diseases two days ahead of schedule, and if she hadn't taken a shortcut across the monument's mall, she would never have been a hostage. And Alec would never have met her, known her, and would never have had to spend two years reliving the sounds of the shots that killed her.

With each step closer he'd come to uncovering the money and power behind the terrorists, Cait's screams had seemed to grow a little dimmer, even if the two sharp reports and her abrupt silence seemed to grow louder in his mind.

And now he discovered she was alive.

The screams, the shots, the sudden cessation of her frantic calling of his name had all been proof enough, but it had been the look in his friends' eyes, that commingled expression of sympathy, wariness and loss that had underscored his knowledge. He'd seen their eyes when he woke. Beyond that, he hadn't wanted to know anything. That, more than anything else, made him dead, as well.

Sending an anonymous sympathy card would have held little or no meaning for Cait's aunt Margaret. He'd seen photos of his fake grave—why would he have wanted to visit Cait's all-too-real resting place? Just to take her flowers, as if on a date they never had?

But he wished to God that he'd done all of those things now. He wished he'd grabbed Jack, Fred or Jorge by the lapels and demanded every last detail of Cait's passing, because *then* he would have known she lived. Then, *he* might have truly lived, not merely survived.

They'd all been there during those dark, touch-and-go early days of recovery. Abiding by company rules—an injured agent working with sensitive material must always be attended by another agent to ensure that no vital information slipped out while under influence of drugs or delirium—and he'd seen one or another of them each time he groggily opened his eyes. Each of his three possibly murdering friends.

Alec hadn't been too clear when he first woke in the hospital. Nights and days, weeks blurred together. Pain was a demon presence that gnawed at his insides, clawed at his chest. But surely one of them had heard him muttering Cait's name, sometimes even waking himself screaming for her. Why hadn't they told him the truth? Why hadn't they just told him she was alive? Why hadn't he asked?

He couldn't remember which of his three friends had been present when he'd finally regained a few of his marbles. The time in the utility closet had seemed like only yesterday to him, but he'd discovered that even the investigation of the hostage situation had already concluded, six full weeks after the fact. The terrorists were judged independents, the FBI was absolved of any possible wrongdoing. And to the world, Alec MacLaine was dead.

The bureau had decided Alec's name was too public for him to be of any use in undercover operations. Jack had explained that Alec had been given a new name, a new past, so that his future would be safer. And, when Alec returned to field work, he'd be better able to go deep under cover.

Alec hadn't given a damn what name they put on his driver's license. Cait was dead. And it was fitting that Alec MacLaine was dead, as well.

He survived, his body healed, he assumed a new name, was useful as a deep-cover agent and eventually wound up in New Mexico, researching land grants by day and seeking revenge by night.

And now he'd discovered the past two years had been a colossal sin of omission. His friends had known about Cait. All they would have had to do was say, "Cait Wilson survived."

Three little words.

Instead, they'd let him believe he'd failed her. Let her die. Had they guessed something had happened to him inside that closet that defied rational rules of behavior? Had his friend who wanted him dead gleaned that his interest in Cait went far beyond mere concern for a fellow human being? Someone had wanted him dead, and he'd lived. Take away what a man wanted most and he was as good as dead. Letting him live as if he *was* dead was the next best thing.

Somebody was going to pay for making the sun go out for two years. Somebody was going to pay very, very dearly.

Alec stood rooted to the floor of his mountain cabin, his current assignment utterly forgotten, telling himself he didn't—couldn't—still possess those inexplicable feelings he'd found with Cait.

And he stared at her living face in full technicolor, seeing the ghost of a woman he'd come closer to believing he could love than any before her. Surrounded by danger, linked together by fate, they'd shared three intimate days of raw intensity. They'd connected in a rare communion of spirit that only the jagged edge of certain death can arrange.

And his own inability to talk about her, to ask about her, combined with the lie of omission had stolen her from him.

"Cait," the interviewer said, leaning nearer, as if closing in for the kill, "Did you actually witness the shootings?"

A dark emotion shadowed Cait's face. "Alec."

"What did you see?"

The camera zoomed in on Cait's face as she frowned heavily, cocking her head as if perplexed by the question. "I saw the terrorists shoot him as they dragged me out of the room."

"You're aware that the FBI's investigation stated you had been unconscious when they arrived on the scene—and at the time of Mr. MacLaine's death."

Alec felt his stomach clench. Why had Cait been unconscious?

Cait shrugged. "It's difficult to remember everything that happened that morning."

The interviewer could read Cait as easily as Alec could; the woman knew Cait was lying, but didn't know what about and, therefore, didn't know what to ask as a follow-up.

"How is it that you weren't called before the Senate Investigation Committee?" the interviewer asked, pouncing.

Cait allowed a half smile. Even through the medium of television, Alec could see the glint of humor. "I was."

"I don't remember seeing you," the woman said.

"You didn't. I gave them a written deposition."

"Was your testimony read aloud to the committee?"

"I don't know."

"Surely, as an eyewitness, you would have been brought forward to tell your story."

"I guess they didn't think what an unconscious woman would have to say would be of any help. The time I was conscious, I was locked in a utility closet and didn't talk to anyone but Alec MacLaine."

Two years later and riveted to the screen, Alec chuckled. But his amusement was short-lived as he listened to Cait's next words.

"You seem to want me to say something dramatic about what happened two years ago, but I can't. A man I barely even knew talked to me, made me laugh and gave me a sense that dying wasn't such a nightmare. Then he was shot and killed right in front of me. That's plenty dramatic in my book."

"You sound as if you loved him," the interviewer said.

Alec held his breath as Cait answered. "I did. With all my heart, and for every minute of those three days. And now he's gone."

Caitlin Leigh Wilson.

Cait was thanked for coming into the studio and the screen faded to a commercial about a breath freshener for those moments when a person wants to be close. And Alec thought about three days without toothpaste, mints or amenities of any kind and a woman who had never once complained or whimpered or acted as if it were anything but the normal state of affairs. And he thought about the past two years living with her ghost.

"She's alive," he said aloud. Then he slapped the Off switch on the front of the television set, spun around and gave a mock jump shot. For the first time in two years his back and shoulders didn't hurt even a little bit. "She's flesh-and-blood, sassy-faced *alive!*" he yelled. And it felt good to hear the timbre of his own shouting voice.

Suddenly the self-imposed loneliness, the emptiness he'd embraced like sackcloth seemed to fall away. Whatever scheme the boys in his office might have hatched up two years ago, whatever darkness had come over them, nothing would ever again be as bleak as thinking Cait was dead.

Alec stopped his restless pacing and frowned. There had been no mention of Cait Wilson in that memorandum he'd stolen. She hadn't spoken before the Senate subcommittee. This was her first interview about the soured situation. It didn't add up. The press would have been all over her.

He'd rashly assumed the lack of her name in the memo was simply an expedient glossing over of the down side of the situation. But now that he'd seen her, watched her, *knew* she was alive, he wondered if the answer wasn't amazingly simple, as simple as the reason he'd been allowed to live: whatever she'd seen that morning couldn't hurt whichever of his three friends had wanted him dead.

Things had not gone as originally planned, but as Cait wasn't part of their scheme, and had apparently been cooperative enough to stay out of the limelight, then she was essentially a nonentity and, therefore, not a threat to the overall cover-up.

It was difficult for Alec to conceive how Cait might be considered a "nonentity." But it wasn't tough to see how her natural reticence—or something else?—had managed to keep her from harm. If someone had gone to such lengths to take him out of the action, it didn't stretch his imagination too far to see that same someone easily taking Cait out if the need should arise.

If he'd been thinking solely in terms of black and white, bad guys and good guys, he could well have imagined that Cait would have been killed within minutes of her apparent escape from the hostage situation. But when it came to longtime friends and colleagues, one couldn't afford the luxury of the lack of shades of gray.

Humankind doesn't think in absolutes. Alec knew that. He was fully aware that egos, needs, motives, desires and ambitions colored every single waking moment of each person out there in the hodgepodge world. To assume that a man wouldn't order another's death while also apparently allowing a young, victimized hostage to live was to fall back into childhood beliefs that the world was comprised of only two types of people: good and bad.

A world with only two types of people wouldn't have need of the CIA, FBI, police, security guards or any of a host of other peacekeeping authorities. It would be a world in fiction only, because people did have multifaceted and highly complex rationales for their behavior.

Alec didn't care, for the moment, *why* Cait had been allowed to live; it was enough to know that in another part of the country she was breathing the same planetary air as he.

And within as short a time as possible, he planned to see her in person.

Chapter 3

The telephone pealed with an urgency only the middle of the night could lend it. Jack King shifted from deep sleep to utter wakefulness and barked his name into the receiver.

"The archangel's flown."

Jack pressed a button on the small box attached to his phone, activating a scrambler. "We're secure," he said. "Now talk to me."

"MacLaine's left New Mexico."

"What!" Jack snarled, having heard his field operative but not believing it, not wanting to believe it. He forced himself to take a deep breath and expel it before asking, "How long ago?" He switched on the light.

"He booked a flight for Atlanta, Georgia, shortly after seven o'clock this evening, or yesterday, rather. We

tailed him to the airport and watched him enter the
boarding chute. The relief in Atlanta says he never got
off.''

"Any connecting flights?"

"No, sir. Straight flight. No stops or layovers.''

Jack realized that some part of him had been expecting and dreading this phone call for almost two years
now. "Anything unusual happen today? Yesterday, I
mean?''

"Nothing, sir. He doesn't go out much, just stays inside his cabin. Pals around with a couple of locals sometimes. He didn't today, though.''

Jack studied the pattern in the floor rug, knowing Alec
MacLaine wasn't "palling around'' with anyone. His
"locals'' were his target in his land-grant investigation.
Jack didn't give them a second thought. Whatever had
propelled Alec out of New Mexico wasn't tied to any
small-time scamming setup.

"As far as we know he didn't talk to anyone today,"
the young agent said.

Jack wondered what Alec might have found out that
afternoon that would cause him to pack up and leave so
abruptly. Had he suspected he was being tailed? If he
had, he might be on the way to discovering the whole
shebang. Jack felt as if an icy hand had grabbed hold of
his ulcer.

"Go on," Jack said.

"He was out of his cabin long enough two weeks ago
that we managed to plant some bugs.''

"And?" Jack asked impatiently. "What have you
heard?''

"Nothing much, sir. Earlier, we just heard the usual
stuff.''

"Like?"

"We heard him fix his dinner. At about five o'clock. At least, that's when his microwave dinged."

Dinged? A new technical word, no doubt. "All right, spare me the nitty-gritty. What else?"

"He worked at his computer for some time, apparently reading, though we occasionally heard some keys typing. He watched the news for a while, then turned it off."

Jack closed his eyes. "Anything visual?"

"No, sir. He has metal venetian blinds. We couldn't make out the key sequencing or access his computer. We speculate by the sounds generated later in the evening that he either uploaded new software or downloaded his own files."

Jack pictured Alec transferring files to disk. It would be like him to leave his computer clean if he was planning something. *Shouldn't be so predictable, pal.* Of course, it was Alec's very predictability that had lulled Jack into a false sense of security. Where the hell had he gone?

"And then he booked the flight for Atlanta."

Why Atlanta? Nothing Alec was working on should take him there, unless something he had found via the computer superhighway had clicked in his head.

Jack's eyes flew open. "Wait a minute. He booked this flight...how? Over the phone?"

"Yes, sir."

Jack shook his head. His boys should have called him at that moment. Alec MacLaine would never have used an open phone line to book a flight he really intended taking. Especially not while in deep cover.

"And you followed him to the airport?"

"Yes, sir, and watched him board the chute."

"How long did you wait after the flight took off?"

"Sir?"

Rookies, Jack thought.

"Uh, we didn't wait, sir."

Had he and Alec ever made such assumptions when they first started? Probably. The cold fist around his ulcer clenched tighter. He popped a cherry-flavored Tums into his mouth and chewed slowly. "You say he watched the news, then turned it off?"

"Yes, sir."

"Before the newscast was over?"

There was a long pause while Jack's two tails conferred with each other. "Before it was over, sir."

They had been intimate with every facet of Alec MacLaine's false life and yet it apparently hadn't fazed them that Alec had turned the news off early. Unless bullets were flying, Alec never interrupted a news program; he faithfully, almost obsessively, watched the full report, local to world news, sports, even weather. Was he aware of this from having known Alec almost fifteen years or was this pair of rookies just asleep at the switch?

"Check out his cabin," Jack said, though he knew with absolute certainty that the young agents wouldn't find any clues. Alec would never leave anything but false leads behind. Sending the agents back there was an unvoiced reprimand for their failure to notify him immediately.

He hung up without saying anything else. He sat on the edge of the bed, aware of the silence, aware of the late hour, and with a sour-stomach surety that everything was falling apart.

He dragged on a robe and padded barefoot down the hallway of his too-empty house into the den and over to the bank of flashing VCRs. Oddly enough, or perhaps ironically, Alec was the one who had got him into the habit of recording all three primary networks' news programs. With use of the remote control device, he rewound the tape on the first one, stopping it just as the credits of one of the national news networks scrolled up the screen. He fast-forwarded through much of it, listening to the first line of each story, checking out the guests and speeding ahead.

He did the same thing to the next tape. It wasn't until he clicked on the third recorder that he saw what had propelled Alec out of his two-year hibernation.

"Damn," he said aloud, freezing the screen to a blurred version of Cait Wilson's face. He frowned, staring at her. "Why couldn't you stay tucked away?"

Loose ends, he thought. They always came back to haunt you.

What was it about this woman? Alec had spent only three days with her, grueling days, granted, but a short time nonetheless. What was it about this particular woman that made a delirious man cry her name out loud, begging her not to die, demanding she come back to him?

Believing she was dead had saved Alec's life, because Alec hadn't given a damn about anything once he woke up. He appeared a whipped man and didn't question his changed circumstances. Seeing the bleak look in his old friend's eyes had nearly made Jack go ahead and tell him the truth. But he hadn't. He couldn't have. Any more than he could have shot Alec himself.

And Jack knew that a man like Alec MacLaine wouldn't stay down for long. A man with Alec's strengths might give in for a while, but he'd never surrender. Alec had spent two years healing, becoming stronger in many ways than he'd been before, because in the days before the shooting, he'd had a whole heart.

In addition to Alec's physical strength and newly ac-
quired cold nature, Jack knew Alec had knowledge he'd
lacked before. He knew this because he was fully aware
of Alec's little raids on the FBI files. He smiled grimly.
He'd even deliberately planted a thing or two for Alec to
filch.

The tight smile faded from Jack's lips. Alec would
know something else, something not available in his lifting of classified information. He'd know by now that
Jack had irretrievably violated the one rule that provided the glue for their relationship: *no lies.*

Without conscious thought Jack hurled the remote
device at the wall with enough force to shatter it. The tape
in the recorder sputtered and the screen went to snow.

He punched in a telephone number and lifted the re-
ceiver to his ear. He was answered on the second ring.
Softly, quietly and with a sense of impending disaster,
Jack gave orders to watch for Alec at both National and
Dulles airports.

Then, very clearly, he recited an address in Chevy
Chase, Maryland. He didn't have to look it up; he'd kept
it in the forefront of his mind for the past two years. A
man always knew the number of his doom.

"Got it, sir."

"If he shows up there, get him. Use any means you
have to. It shouldn't be too difficult. He's not expecting
anyone to know where he is."

"Sir?"

Jack turned his gaze from the shattered bits of black
plastic on the den floor; the devastated remote reminded
him too much of his now-shattered friendship with Alec
MacLaine. He rubbed his sore eyes. He was too old for
this and so damned tired.

"Oh, just get him."

Chapter 4

Saturday, November 10, 3:30 a.m. EST

Some noise, or perhaps an edgy, neck-tingling awareness that things were not as they should be, woke Cait from an uneasy sleep. She lay perfectly still, straining to hear unfamiliar sounds outside, inside, upstairs and down. She heard nothing, but couldn't shake the feeling that something wasn't right.

Several seconds passed without a single rattle to underscore her illusive anxiety and yet her heart continued to beat too rapidly. She let her mouth fall open to breathe even more quietly.

Her eyes raked the dark bedroom and she studied each piece of furniture for movement, for some sign that intruders were present. The bulk against the wall wasn't two men, only her mother's old dresser. The hulking shadow in the corner was simply one of her two easy chairs, this one with a stack of folded laundry resting on its seat. The clothes hanging in the closet were just suits and dresses, not felons filled with murderous intent.

Still the uncomfortable sensation of "not right" persisted. She sat up, hugging the covers to her chest, listening with sharp tension. She'd felt no transition from her rough sleep to full alarm. She didn't hear a repeat of whatever sound had jarred her from her dreams, but she remained wide-eyed with unaccustomed fear.

Two years ago Cait had learned in three short days to trust her instincts about many, many things. She trusted them still. Without knowing exactly why, but relying on those hard-to-define natural gifts, she swung her legs from the bed. She pulled an emerald green satin robe from the bedpost. The house was plenty warm, but she'd read enough on fear to understand that, crazy as it sounded, a feeling of vulnerability could be alleviated by nothing more than a see-through scarf.

She carefully checked the hallway and listened outside one of the other two bedroom doors before pushing it open slightly. In the glow from the night-light, Cait could see that her daughter had rolled to her side. She softly crossed the room and repositioned Allie's blanket over her, though her fuzzy pajama suit was probably sufficient.

"It was that interview," she whispered. "I shouldn't have done it. See what a little fame will bring you? A grand case of the heebie-jeebies."

As she cautiously stepped into the hallway she worked to convince herself that if she hadn't agreed to appear on television that evening she would still be safely and *soundly* sleeping in her wonderfully comfortable bed.

"They promised they wouldn't ask any questions about that time," she muttered. She sneered at her own naiveté. Why else would they have wanted her on the program? Sure, they showed a clip or two of her rescue software, but in the half-hour wait before airtime, the producers of the show had made it perfectly obvious they didn't see any possible need for such a tool.

She didn't blame them. They weren't police, fire fighters, or rescue workers. What would the average person care about door accesses, tensor strengths of arches or doorways? But trap that same Joe beneath a pile of rubble and that person would be praying somebody knew the building's strength ratios.

Her little scenarios, as the producer had referred to her program data, helped rescue people. Helped train people on what to expect in an emergency situation. She could have given them a perfect example: two people, two utter strangers, different backgrounds and sexes, throw them into a hostile, dangerous situation. Mix well. In her program they would either work together to find a way out or they would fight until neither spoke to the other. In reality... they'd talked about dream houses.

She hesitated as she left her daughter's room, torn between a desire to close the bedroom door and an equally strong urge to leave it open so she could hear Allie. She left it open the tiniest crack and proceeded in her search for whatever had her nerves a-jangle.

She peeked in the second bedroom as well, flicking on the light for a second, taking the empty room in at a glance. Then as she doused the light, she stared deeply into every dark corner, a prescient sense of danger keeping her utterly silent, moving without so much as a rustle.

Nothing was amiss and yet everything seemed wrong.

She turned for the stairs, hesitating at the top, groping for the railing and the light switch simultaneously. She stood there for a moment, cocking her head, straining to hear whatever it was that held her poised for trouble. When she flipped the switch and soft, muted light gave a peach-tinged glow to the stairwell, she should have sighed in relief, but instead tensed even more, as if the light itself represented the danger she anticipated.

Still hearing nothing unusual, she nonetheless proceeded down the first step with extreme caution, bending slightly to peek through the decorative rail supports, seeing nothing in the darkened living room, but half certain something waited for her there anyway.

"This is ridiculous," she muttered finally, but still jumping at the sound of her own low voice. She pictured headlines in the Sunday papers—Woman Scares Self To Death By Talking Aloud. She marched down the carpeted stairs making as much racket as the plush material would allow.

She flicked on the switch for the living room lamps and whirled around, prepared for someone to leap out at her. She was only marginally less nervous as she did the same thing in the dining room. Only the kitchen and garage left.

Thunk.

She froze, hand halfway to the kitchen light switch. For half a minute she was paralyzed by another series of thunderous sounds before realizing it was her own furiously beating heart. She thrust the light switch downward with enough force to hurt her hand. She *needed* the light, as if the fluorescents in her kitchen would have the power to roust any marauding intruder.

And then she heard something else. Unfamiliar yet recognizable. A noise like something she might have heard in a dream or even read about in a book. It was a high-pitched whine, not like the grind of a saw, but higher, the piercing buzz a hummingbird makes when diving at a feeder. But unnatural, metallic. Different.

Whatever it was, whatever atavistic chord it struck in her, she froze, staring wild-eyed at the front door. The sound had come from outside, and some part of her half expected the source to come whirring into her house at any moment.

Instead, shattering the ghastly silence, tires squealed a furious protest outside her house and she heard a car zoom away. Someone *had* been outside. Had been there and left. She felt such a wave of relief wash over her that she had to put her hand out to the countertop to hold herself upright.

It was probably someone from next door. The neighbors, Sean and Delia Dimwits, the undynamic duo, were probably fighting again. They did it on a far too regular basis.

Something had been wrong, all right, but not with her home, not directed at her. Half laughing at herself, she poured a glass of chilled water and drank it down, willing her hands to stop shaking. She clicked off the kitchen light, walked through the dining room and darkened it, as well.

In the shadows and in the act of pulling her hand away from the living room switch, she jumped a full three inches when the front windows suddenly turned bright. The outside floodlight, activated by a motion detector, had turned on, lighting the porch, the outside and her windows.

The abrupt change from night to day right outside her house, reanimated her and she stumbled on rubbery legs to the front door. She was shaking so hard she had to lay both palms against the door in order to lean close enough to see through the peephole.

She saw her slender porch, the two short cement steps leading down to the sidewalk that stretched to the street.

Her eye pressed to the peephole, her hands flat on the door, she felt the wood shudder. Her heart missed a full beat and she jerked away from the door as if it were on fire.

"Cait . . . ?"

Strangely disembodied, the voice that called her name seemed to come from behind her and she pivoted to stare through her darkened dining room at her night black kitchen.

"Cait . . . ?"

No. Whoever called her had to be the cause of the floodlights coming on, was responsible for the shudder of her door.

And whoever it was knew her name.

The doorknob didn't move. The door didn't rattle. And nothing whined outside. But she knew someone waited outside her door, waited for her to invite danger inside.

She crept back to the door, lightly resting her fingers against the flat surface. She had to force herself to press her eye to the peephole. She couldn't see a thing and realized with a jagged flash of terror that something—some*one*—was blocking the tiny lens. Someone was leaning against her door. She was separated from whoever was out there by an inch of wood and metal. Nothing more.

Just then the person against her door stepped back a pace, allowing her a glimpse of his face. Cait felt the blood leaving hers. Her legs, liquid before, turned cold and leaden.

"No," she whispered. What she was seeing was impossible. She'd always believed in ghosts. She'd just never expected to see one.

This ghost turned full face to the door then, as if he knew she was on the other side of the viewing hole.

Alec MacLaine.

Dead, buried. Mourned by an entire country.

Alec . . . dark, curling hair, thick black eyebrows, eyes the color of liquid cobalt. Lips that could incite a riot. Back from the grave and standing on her doorstep.

Where her heart had pounded too furiously before, it now seemed to give a pitiful, tiny jerk and then stop altogether. She couldn't breathe. The only sign of life within her came from her suddenly wildly shaking hands. She wished she could simply faint. Or wake up from this new twist in an otherwise familiar nightmare.

Alec.

A low moan escaped her lips. It seemed to come from her very soul.

She wondered if the noise she'd heard, the odd and unrepeated vibration that woke her, had been a gun in the hands of robbers. That was it. She'd been shot. And died. And Alec's ghost had come for her.

He pressed the doorbell, making her jolt two inches when it went off directly over her head. He winced and looked behind him, as if afraid the sound of the bell would wake the neighborhood. She bit her lip in reaction. Surely ghosts wouldn't wince or ring doorbells in the wee hours of the morning. He craned his neck to look at the empty street in front of her house. He didn't have a car, at least, none that she could see.

She understood several things in lightning succession: Alec was really alive. However improbably and impossibly, he was on her doorstep. He had apparently arrived by taxi, which accounted for the screech of tires. And the whine she'd heard was probably feedback from the taxi's radio. That was why the sound had seemed familiar— she'd heard it on television a thousand times. She perceived all this, but could make no sense of it; all of it, everything, was simply incomprehensible.

"Cait?" he called again softly. Staring at him, seeing him mouth her name, she realized she recognized his voice.

He pressed the doorbell again. This time, despite her convulsive start, she was galvanized into action. She yanked back the locks and jerked the door open, wrenching at the knob with cold, shaking hands.

This was no dream, no nightmare. He was really there.

"Alec," she breathed.

He stared at her blankly for a moment, as if he hadn't expected to see her on the other side of the door, or, making her quake inside, as if he'd forgotten what she looked like, then he pushed her back into the house, following her only to swiftly shove the door into place.

As if it were his home, he tossed an overnight bag to the floor, slapped the locks into place and, with two long strides, crossed to her front windows. He stood with his back to the wall and pulled the curtains back a mere inch to peer outside.

Only then did Cait see that he held a gun in his hand.

She felt as if her feet had grown roots and she was firmly planted to her living room floor. "You're... dead," she whispered.

The outside floods, timed for the minimum setting, abruptly cut off, plunging them in shadow. The only light in the room filtered down from the stairway.

"I came as soon as I knew. I suspected someone might not want me around, but I didn't dream they'd follow me here."

"I don't understand—"

"God, Cait, I'm so sorry," he continued, ignoring her interruption, still looking out the window.

"What?" Like his presence in the middle of the night, like his very existence, his words carried no meaning for Cait. He might as well have been speaking Latin for all the sense he made.

"Get some things together. I'll find us a place where we can be safe tonight."

"Safe," Cait repeated, frowning. She still stood in the exact same spot where he'd thrust her upon his entry. She stared at him, grappling with the realization that he wasn't dead, was in her house in the middle of the night—two years after she'd gone to his *funeral*—and was talking to her as if he'd run into a little trouble while going to the corner grocery for a pack of cigarettes.

She hadn't seen him for *two* years. Two years, filled with hard work, tough times, lonely wakeful nights, and a million unanswered questions. She'd last seen him shot and bleeding on the cloth they'd used as a bed.

But she didn't say any of this, couldn't have spoken if her very life depended on it. She only looked at him, seeing a gray streak in the hair at his temple, his dark mane longer, curling at his collar. Had he always seemed so imposing? Had his shoulders been so broad two years ago?

She thought she'd remembered every single detail about him, but staring at him now, she found she'd forgotten how square his chin was, how chiseled his cheeks. He had an odd tan line across his cheeks, as if he wore a mask on the lower half of his face during the day. He looked harder, as though an anger had blossomed in him somewhere, a quiet, rough fury that he'd learned to take energy from rather than letting it go.

Maybe that illusion came from the gun he held so purposefully in his steady hand.

Something in the grim set of his mouth stayed her thousands of questions. She clamped her quivering lips together, trying so hard not to let him see how thoroughly his return from the grave unnerved her.

"What—?" she managed to whisper.

He didn't answer, his attention focused intently on the street.

The impossibility of his presence warred with a peculiar sense that some corner of the world had righted itself, that a dreadful mistake had been corrected. *Alec had come back.*

She had to force air to make her voice loud enough for him to hear. "What . . . is . . . going on?"

He turned to look at her and did a slight double take, as if he was only just then seeing her. His eyes roamed her face, her satin ensemble, as if she were the person—not he—who had mysteriously come back from a grave.

Then his look changed from the rough are-you-the-same-person? appraisal to a longing she'd never seen on his face before. Not once during those three days. It was a hunger that didn't address the chemistry that had flared so naturally between them. The look encompassed broken promises and lost dreams and a well of bitterness so deep it couldn't possibly be plumbed. She suspected he was unaware how fiercely he stared at her.

She shut her eyes. Surely she was asleep. Dreaming as she had so many times before that Alec had come back to her, that he'd lived, that the reports of his death, the shots she'd seen lodge in his chest, had been an incredible, colossal mistake: *No, no, he's fine,* someone's kindly voice would say, *just a little scratch. Alec, dead? Heavens, no.*

And in her dreams he would touch her face in that distinctively tender way, caressing her with the backs of his fingers, trailing the line of her cheeks with his thumbs.

"Ah, Cait..." he would say.

"Cait...?"

She opened her eyes. He wasn't beside her, hand lifted to stroke her face, but was standing beside her window, watching her warily, gun pointed toward her new carpet. She wasn't sleeping; she was awake and Alec MacLaine was alive.

"I saw you s-shot in the chest," she said raggedly. "I saw the bullets hit you three times." The exact number of times he'd been shot suddenly seemed very important.

She saw a muscle flex in his jaw. She remembered feeling it jerk beneath her hand two years ago. It happened when he was angry. Or when he was cresting the tide of passion. She felt a wave of heat rush through her body at the memory. A feeling that was followed by cold confusion.

"I know, Cait. I'm so sorry," he said. His voice held a jagged note. She couldn't read his expression; it carried too many nuances. Regret? Apology? Something else. Anger?

She persisted with her own thoughts, needing to understand the paradox apparently confronting her in her own living room, "I saw you lying on that c-cloth. Bleeding to death."

"I know," he said, his tone raw, the way it had sounded that last morning. "It doesn't matter now."

"Doesn't matter?" she asked, aghast.

He let the curtain twitch back into place and stood perfectly still, not two yards away from her, staring at her as if she were a keg of unstable dynamite. His shoulders flexed and Cait knew he would move forward. Still struggling to understand, to fathom this incredible miracle, she held her hand to stop him from coming any closer. If he touched her, her confusion would be total.

Part of her ached to have him close the distance between them so she could slip into his arms and stay there forever, clinging to the dream that had sustained her for two long years. But another part of her, a wholly unfamiliar rock-hard self, held back, afraid, not of him, perhaps, *never of Alec,* but of whatever he represented with his lowered gun—a *gun*—and his incomprehensible talk of people following him to her house.

Even as she desperately tried thinking of him as the "old" Alec, the man who drove terror from a dark closet, who had held her in his arms and kissed away fear…she suddenly remembered, coldly recalled that this was also the man who hadn't told her he was with the FBI, that she'd had to discover that little tidbit after finding out he was dead. This "new" Alec was a perfect stranger to her, and a lot less than perfect at that.

"Ah, Cait…" he murmured, holding out his free hand.

"Alec," she whispered, agonized. Confused. She unconsciously slid forward a step.

Yes, and he's danger walking, that other part of herself cautioned.

But he's back! He's here.

And he left you alone once before, didn't he? He allowed you to think he was dead.

"You have no idea how very good it is to see you," he said slowly and with unsmiling, heavy irony as if he really had come back from his nonexistent grave. He slid his gun beneath his jacket.

She couldn't say anything. Was it good to see him? How could she answer her own inner question? Was it good to see the sun after two years of darkness? Was it good to see a dead man alive again?

That inner voice she was beginning to despise spoke up again. *He lied to you. He abandoned you. You didn't mourn a man, you mourned a fantasy. This man is a total stranger. He always was.*

"I've thought about you every day for two years," he said.

An icy sensation trickled through her body as that mysterious other self surfaced, the self born two years before at the precise moment she witnessed his murder, and nurtured in the dark nights in between that day and now.

"Cait—?"

The chill working through her coalesced to a freezing, frigid anger. She waved her hand to halt his words. She advanced another single step, leaning forward slightly, suddenly furious, terrified and implacable in her deep sense of betrayal.

"I went to your *funeral*. I *cried* at your funeral. I cried every damned day for six months. I thought I would never *stop* crying."

With each word she slid forward another notch, as if her anger propelled her and not her feet.

"Darling—"

"Don't call me that!" she snapped. "You don't have any right to use endearments. You've let me think for two years that you *died* trying to save my life! *Died.* Do you know what that does to a person's head?"

"I know, Cait. Believe me, I know."

"You don't have the slightest inkling of what that feels like! You couldn't or you wouldn't have put me through it."

"Cait, I *do* know," he said, his voice harsh.

"I still have nightmares, Alec. Nightmares. And fantasies, my God, the torture I've gone through wondering, asking myself over and over if we could have had something together if only you'd lived...."

Aghast at her own words, at the raw admission of her pain, and at the look of stunned guilt on his face, something in Cait snapped, broke like a brittle twig.

Tears sprang from her eyes like pellets. Without conscious thought she closed the last few inches separating them, her fists raised and her arms flailing. She beat at his chest with each word, "You...let...me...think... you...were...*dead!*"

For a moment, as if accepting the guilt, Cait continued to ineffectually slap at his rock-hard chest, then he clamped both his arms around her and held her still against him. As she'd wanted. And as she hated herself for wanting.

She struggled against him, wriggling and thrashing her head.

"Damn it, Cait, stop it!"

Holding her with one arm, he raised his other hand to press her head against his thundering heart.

"Cait. Sh-h-h. I'm sorry, Cait. It's not what you think. It's not at all what you think."

Cait felt the anger slipping from her with each stroke of his hand against her hair. Her tears, born of a deep well of anger, were stymied by his gentleness, his apology, his assurance that she wasn't aware of cause, reasons or facts.

"Sh-h-h. It's okay, Cait. It'll be all right, now." He held her, soothing her, gentling her, stroking her hair, her shoulders, taking her back in time with his touch, bringing her back to the present with his palpable, remarkable reappearance.

His hand caressed her hair, her neck, her shoulders with exquisite tenderness, an almost studious lack of passion, betraying how deeply the closeness affected him, as well. How many times she'd longed to be held just this way, stroked, gentled, reassured. And how many times had she wanted this melting sensation of pure contact, not just contact with anyone... with Alec.

To touch Alec, to feel that muscle in his jaw leap beneath her sensitive fingertips, to feel his heart hammering against her ear, his hands tangled in her hair, these all could comprise a two-year definition of paradise.

Beneath his touch, pressed tightly against him now, confused but quiescent, Cait felt the last of her sustaining anger drain from her. She reluctantly stirred in his arms.

"Tell me what's going on, Alec. Tell me why you're here, why you let me believe you were dead." Her voice was steady now, even if her tone was flatter than usual.

He met her gaze with slow, questioning intensity, as if gauging how much she was ready to take, not as if she were volatile any longer, but as though she might sink to the floor in a parody of an old-fashioned swoon.

"Just tell me, Alec. I have a right to know. More right than you can guess."

He frowned at this, but didn't pursue it. "I never meant for you to be hurt, Cait."

She didn't try to pull all the way out of his arms. It felt strange to stand within his grasp, drawn to him, yet oddly aloof. "What is going on, Alec? Where have you been?"

He drew a deep breath and raised a hand to her cheek, cupping it gently. "All this time I've thought *you* were dead."

Chapter 5

Cait was grateful Alec held her; she might have fallen to her knees otherwise. "What? Why did you think *I* was dead?"

He shook his head and his grip tightened on her arms. "It doesn't matter now, Cait." He drew her into his embrace, cradling her against his chest, lowering his jaw to her temple to press a long, gentle kiss against her sensitive skin. "All that matters is that it wasn't true. Oh, God, it wasn't true."

"I don't understand any of this," she said, resisting the urge to press her own lips to his shoulder. It felt so right, so impossibly perfect to be in his arms again. She raised her hand to his muscled arm and felt him tense at the same moment she encountered something hot and wet on his jacket sleeve.

"It's just a scratch," he said. "Someone got me just before I made it to the porch. I didn't recognize him and he drove away."

Blood. He'd been shot. She hadn't seen him for two years and he'd shown up in the middle of the night with a gunshot wound.

She didn't try to pull out of his grasp, and with far more calm than she felt she asked, "Are you going to tell me what's going on?"

"I read a memorandum last week that suggests the terrorists that held us two years ago were hired to kill me," he said, his rich voice curiously devoid of emotion.

"I see," she said. And she wasn't lying to him. Despite the findings of the Senate subcommittee investigation all that time ago, she'd often wondered if Alec hadn't been the real target. Why else would they have so coldly murdered him—correction, badly wounded him—yet let her live?

And she had wanted to continue living, so had kept her mouth shut tight. Nothing she could have said would have brought Alec back, and she'd soon discovered other excellent reasons to keep quiet. So, she'd stuck to her "I was unconscious" story and, amazingly, no one had ever challenged her. Until that interview, and even that small challenge was dropped.

"Do you see, Cait?"

"I think so," she answered, and told him why.

When she'd finished he nodded and stroked her hair. "What a hell of a mess."

"They're still after you, then?"

"Apparently."

"Why? They could have killed you anytime in the past two years. Why wait until now?" She almost smiled at the sheer callousness of the question, but this was Alec she was talking with; she could say *anything* to Alec. Or she could have once.

"I was out of the picture. That's the only reason I can come up with—at least for now."

Cait sensed there was more to his theory than he was revealing, but decided not to ask about the past, only the present. "And you're not out of the picture anymore?"

"Not since I saw you on the news tonight." His arms tightened around her.

"You really thought I was dead?"

"And buried."

"Did someone tell you that?"

"It was more a matter of not telling me you were alive."

Cait mulled this over and decided against pointing out a glaring parallel. "We should do something about your arm."

"Not just yet," he said. "Let me hold you a minute longer. Ah-h-h, Cait."

She closed her eyes in exquisite pleasure. She'd never believed she would hear just those words spoken in just that way again. When he lowered his lips to her forehead she wanted to raise her face, to taste him for the first time in two years.

Instead, for reasons she couldn't begin to explain, she tilted her head downward, avoiding a contact she'd craved every minute of each passing day. She'd learned to trust her instincts all that time ago, and she wasn't going to stop now. Whatever trouble cruised around with him on this November night would have to wait until his arm was bandaged and until he'd explained why he'd allowed an entire country to mourn his loss.

He let her go easily. Too easily, she thought. She glanced at him then away. "Come on into the kitchen with me," she said. "I'll patch up your arm."

"Cait—" he said, stopping her.

"Yes?"

The muted lighting in the room made it difficult for her to read his expression. He didn't say anything for several seconds, then shrugged slightly. "Look, you have to believe me when I tell you I never meant to bring trouble here. It's the last thing in the world I'd want. I thought I'd covered my tracks. I never so much as suspected they'd guess I'd come here. Or maybe they just followed me from the airport. I don't know."

"It's all right, Alec," she lied.

"No. It's not. In fact, it couldn't be worse."

She frowned a question.

"Whoever it is, they'll be back, Cait."

"Let me patch your arm, then you can go."

"You don't understand, Cait. I'm not going to leave you here. They know I've been here. They'll believe you'll know where I'm going."

Her frown deepened and her heart seemed to be attempting to escape from her body. "I can't believe this is happening," she said.

"I know," he said, so calmly and quietly that it angered her a little. "But I'd feel better if we got out of here."

"Out of here," she repeated. "Leave here in the middle of the night."

"It'll be morning in a few hours."

"But—"

"I'll find us someplace safe."

She knew what he was saying and guessed at many things he wasn't. But he didn't understand. She wasn't the same woman she'd been two years ago. She had other things, other *people* to consider now. She could only stare at him, not so much in fear of the ramifications but in denial that they could touch her.

"I could be wrong, Cait. Let's hope I am. But I'm damned if I'll take chances with your life. Not now that I've found you again."

She realized in a blinding flash that he'd only seen her on the news. He didn't know anything about her. He hadn't asked about Allie. It was safe to assume he didn't know about her, safe to believe he didn't have so much as a glimmer of an idea that a child slept upstairs.

His child. Their child.

A wave of undiluted horror washed over her. In her fantasies, in the millions of dreams where Alec came back, it had been easy to tell him about Allie, he'd somehow known a little girl waited to call him Daddy.

"Cait, I'm serious—"

What was she to do? Take Allie and flee with Alec into the unknown darkness, not even knowing why? She shook her head. "No, Alec. I can't."

"Cait—"

"No. I'm not going a single step until I make some sense of this," she said, her voice trembling.

He looked away from her as if seeking an answer from her dim living room, and something in his shadowed expression made her realize that he truly didn't fully understand what was happening. That frightened her more than anything else.

And it made her next words colder than she might have wished. "Start with your supposed death and continue from there."

"The FBI faked my death."

"No kidding," she retorted. "Somehow, I managed to guess that much, Alec. Give me a break. I'm stunned to see you alive, but it doesn't make me brain-dead. What I want to know is *why?* Why fake a death?"

"I told you earlier, I had to be out of the picture."

"Why?"

"Because I knew too much?"

"Are you asking me?"

"What?"

"Are you playing that game where you answer a question with a question?"

"Cait, damn it."

"Statement. You're out."

He stared at her as if she'd suddenly sprouted snakes from her hair. "You've changed."

"Of course I've changed. Two years is a long time, Alec. I thought you were dead. I went on with my life. A life you've had absolutely nothing to do with. And then you show up on my doorstep with a—a *bullet* in your arm—"

"It's just a scratch. There isn't any bullet in me."

"Excuse me. You show up with a bullet *wound* on your arm and you tell me that someone's after you, and they're going to come back, and you imply that if I don't leave with you right now they're going to torture me into telling them what I probably wouldn't have known in the first place. Have I got just a little of the picture here?"

To her utter amazement, he grinned. A totally, wholly disarming, memory-warping grin. "You were always good at that."

They'd had too little time together for him to know if she'd *always* been good at anything. The very word *always* implied an interwoven past, a contiguous time spent together. Still, she had to ask, "At what?"

"At taking the most outrageous, terrible thing and turning it into a joke."

"A *joke?*" she asked, shocked. "I wasn't joking, Alec. I can't do this."

His brows furrowed. "Do what?"

"Do *what?*" she asked, so astounded she literally had to walk off her stupefaction. "Danger. Bullets. Lovers returning from the dead. Let's take those for starters, shall we?"

He lifted his hand as if he would reach for her, only to drop it to his side again. The gesture stopped her, despite the lack of contact. Aching for him to touch her, she stayed three inches out of his grasp and studied him, trying to glean any semblance of understanding.

His perplexed expression and his tense body let her know more clearly than any words that she had to listen to him, that she had to get Allie out of the house.

"I don't know how much time we have, Cait," he said, unknowingly underscoring her thoughts.

"We never have any time," she said.

He stared at her for a long moment before stepping within kissing distance of her. "And if we don't get a move on, we won't have any time ever."

She could feel his warm breath on her skin, he was so close. And his eyes never wavered from hers as he let her see he was saying nothing but the absolute truth. The "scratch" on his arm, the one dripping blood onto her carpet, confirmed that grim truth.

"Who's after you, Alec?"

"If I'm right, it's one of three friends of mine."

"Pretty crummy friends."

He grinned crookedly. Bitterly. "One of them is."

"And you don't know which one."

"That's right. Can we go now?"

He'd said, *If I'm right,* which led her to assume there was a possibility that he wasn't. "Are these supposed friends colleagues of yours in the bureau?" she asked slowly, understanding beginning to filter in.

He looked surprised. "Yes."

"But why would they be after *you?* You're one of them. Or at least, you were. Are you still?"

He nodded to her last question, but didn't answer her others. She understood why; he didn't have those answers.

He reached for her then, resting his broad palms on her shoulders. She could feel the heat through the satiny material of her nightgown. He lifted one hand to her cheek and traced the curve of her jaw with his thumb. "Hurry, Cait."

But standing in the dimly lit living room, feeling the touch of a man she'd truly mourned as dead, she found she could scarcely breathe, let alone move. She had to tell him about Allie. Needed to tell him. And couldn't find the words.

His hand enfolded her shoulder, squeezed it gently. "Cait. God knows we need to talk." He slowly drew her closer. She didn't resist. "There's a lot I don't understand, and we can go over it together. And there's..." He trailed off, his eyes boring into hers. His mouth worked, his gaze faltered. "But we've got to get going. *Now.*"

His hands seemed to burn her skin. She might as well have been naked. His grip shifted, turned to caress instead of grasp. Unconsciously she tilted her head to the side, allowing him access.

He'd said they needed to hurry, and she believed him. But he didn't release her shoulders and she didn't pull away. His thumb traced a small circle against her collarbone. She closed her eyes, the memory of his touch merging with reality.

"You are so very beautiful, Cait."

This time she didn't lower her face, didn't try to hide from his kiss. His firm lips were amazingly soft and his tongue liquid velvet. She couldn't withhold a moan as she leaned into him. A sharp, jagged-edged surge of pure desire rioted through her, making her knees buckle, her body arch into him. Danger, a secret baby, two years of loneliness . . . they were swept away in the mindless need for his touch. God, how she'd missed him.

That strange and cold inner voice so vocal earlier made a few squawking protests, but subsided completely as his hands drove into her hair. His palms pressed against her cheeks, and he pulled her even closer, deepening his kiss.

She gave in to the kiss, the feel of his hot lips against hers, his solid body pressing into her. His hands grasped her waist and pulled her even closer as though to draw her inside him.

She tasted him and recognized the sweet-salty tang unique to him, drank in his scent and reveled in the feel of his hands in her hair, at her back, his chest beneath her fingers. She heard his ragged breathing and knew it matched her own.

Not such a stranger, after all. Two years gone, but the chemistry hadn't altered one iota. What did it mean? And soon she had no thoughts at all. She seemed to be floating inches above the ground, her body alive, gloriously, wondrously alive.

Far away, in another reality, a baby cried.

The feel of Alec's lips—moist, hot, demanding—drowned the single cry, allowed her to lose the link she had with that voice.

Another cry, more demanding. Pay attention to *me*.

Reluctantly, more reluctantly than he would ever know, Cait dazedly pulled back a bit and turned her face toward the landing at the top of the stairs, listening, trying to find her way back to the ground, craving the touch of the fantasy, needing to attend her daughter in the very concrete present.

Alec held on to her, stopping her, blocking her automatic departure. He frowned and tilted his head in her view. "What's that?"

Cait had thought that all she had to do was tell him and they'd run out into the night together, escaping danger, neatly rearranging their lives and realigning their fates. But like everything else about Alec, simple explanations were a fantasy, too.

"My...d-daughter," she said faintly.

"Your *what?*"

"You didn't know."

"Hell, no, I didn't know. I thought you were dead, remember? How would I know you had a...a daughter?" He didn't sound angry but he looked as though he were poised to strike or waiting for a blow to fall.

Somewhat angrily, she realized he didn't even so much as suspect the truth. She tried pulling away from him, but he didn't let her go. He held her almost absently, his mind obviously churning furiously while his daughter continued her demand for company.

"Cait?"

She wouldn't meet his eyes, wouldn't let him read her thoughts.

"You have a baby?" he asked incredulously. He sounded as if she'd just picked up a two-by-four and slammed it into his head. "I don't... How—? I mean, when?"

The baby's wails escalated and Cait shrugged free and started up the stairs.

His hand shot out and circled her upper arm, checking her flight. She didn't look back at him.

"Are you married, Cait?" His voice was hoarse. Raw. "Is someone else...here?"

Cait knew the question he'd almost asked didn't relate to anyone else's presence in her home, but rather if there was anyone in her life at all.

"Yes . . . no. I'm not married."

"But someone else is here?"

"I told you. My daughter. I've got to go to her," Cait said, desperate for escape and pulled by her baby's cries.

"Ma-ma!" the baby called out, her little voice never clearer than at this moment.

Alec's hand squeezed painfully, and Cait suspected unconsciously.

"Mama?" he asked. "She's old enough to talk?" He pulled her back around to face him. The muscle in his jaw jumped and his eyes blazed with sharp, stunned comprehension. "How old is your baby, Cait?"

In her fantasies, in the dreams in which Alec hadn't died, in which they'd moved to that big house in the country with the big oaks and the picnic table, Alec had known every detail of her daughter's life—her birth, her first tooth, her first stumbling step.

Staring straight across at him now, seeing by his face that he could read the truth in hers, she could only think that life wasn't fair, that some cruel and twisted fate had stolen so much from both of them.

"How old is your baby?" he asked again. He seemed unaware his fingers were digging into her arms.

"She," Cait corrected.

"How *old* is *she*, Cait?"

Cait took a deep breath and told him the raw truth. "She's fourteen months old."

Alec let Cait slip from his nerveless hands. He didn't try to stop her as she fled up the stairwell. He stood alone on the first floor of Cait's house, his thoughts as murky as the gloom surrounding him.

When he'd first heard the baby cry, with Cait molded against him, her body still warm from sleep, the emerald satin liquid beneath his hands, he'd half wondered if he wasn't hearing things. Almost immediately, the notion that Cait might be married flashed through his mind like a bolt of too bright, jagged lightning.

But the look on Cait's face. Good God, that *look*. Surely he'd misunderstood. Surely his supposition was wrong.

The baby crying upstairs—*Cait's baby*—was fourteen months old. It didn't take a math wizard to wade through the simple subtraction process to discover the baby's possible conception date. Three days, two years ago. Three days when they'd been certain to die. Time spent with no thought of protection because there had been zero chance of survival and ramifications only applied when a future was involved.

But they had lived.

And Cait had had a baby fourteen months ago, while he was still suffering through physical therapy. Had she cried out in pain? Had she cursed him? Would their individual pain have been less had each known the other lived?

The baby stopped crying and the house seemed unnaturally silent.

Cait's pale face, her quivering lips, even the odd apology in her eyes had all told him more clearly than any direct words could have done that the baby upstairs was his.

A little girl. A daughter.

His daughter.

Whatever look of shock he'd seen on Cait's face when he burst into her home had to be nothing compared to what must be plastered on his own features right now. He was assaulted by a myriad of unrelated emotions ranging from a stinging guilt to an almost embarrassed pride. His lips twitched in what might be considered a hysterical grin while his fingers flexed in helpless restlessness.

On numb legs he steered up the stairs, taking them as an old man might do, one careful step at a time. A softly glowing lamp beside an opened bedroom door beckoned him and made his heart pound with fear greater than any he'd ever known before.

He heard Cait murmuring softly, and entered the lamp-golden bedroom in time to see her lowering her lips to the baby's soft crown of dark curls. Somewhere deep inside him a fist took hold and wrenched open a door he'd believed nailed shut.

Cait held the baby in her arms, slowly rocking from foot to foot, ethereal in her satin robe, soft light creating a halo around her blond hair. She'd never looked more beautiful than she did cradling the dark-haired child in her arms. Her expression was soft with an aching tenderness and mirrored the deepest of loves.

He didn't know how long he remained silent in the doorway. It felt like seconds and at the same time, the moment seemed to stretch into infinity, a memory forged into his mind with blades of hot iron. As long as he lived, he knew he would never forget his first sight of Cait holding her—their—daughter.

He had to clear a suddenly aching and full throat before he could speak. "What's her name?"

Cait looked up from her contemplation of the baby, the tenderness still sculpted on her features, a soft smile still teasing her parted lips. For the fraction of a second

Alec knew what it felt like to have such love directed at him, then her chin lifted, and a wariness, perhaps even a fear, stole into her green eyes.

"Allie," she said.

"What?" he asked blankly.

"Her name. It's Allie. I called her Allie Elaine Wilson."

Allie Elaine. Alec MacLaine.

Alec had to close his eyes against the proof he hadn't needed. Unbidden came that picture of a mantel in a desperate dream house, a little girl's school photos.

Dark haired like him.

Chapter 6

"She looks like you," Cait said, unknowingly echoing his thoughts.

Alec opened his eyes to see tears standing in hers. He glanced down at the baby before Cait could see that his own eyes were misting over.

"Allie," he murmured, tasting his baby's name on his tongue for the first time. The name felt right, carried a hint of spice and nostalgia.

The little girl, still a newborn in Alec's inexperienced eyes, turned her wide blue gaze in his direction. Her lips, rosy and pouty like her mother's, pursed, and a tiny frown creased her brow. Alec found himself holding his breath. She seemed to study him with the serious contemplation of a judge in criminal court, then, in a tran-

sition as swift as the change from warm to hot, her baby
lips parted in a broad, toothy smile.

Alec's heart turned over and he found he could breathe
again. Unconsciously, he grinned back, and the smile felt
odd on his face, as if it didn't belong there, as if the
muscles needed to create the grin had atrophied years
before.

How could his friends have stolen this strange and
wonderful feeling from him? By not telling him Cait was
alive, by letting him believe his own senses, they'd not
only robbed him of the potential of Cait, they'd stripped
him of having known he had a child. A daughter. Allie.

For a moment, gripped in the struggle between anger
at his friends and a far more powerful wonder at meeting his own daughter, Alec had to speculate what might
have happened in his life if he hadn't watched the news
earlier that night. Would he never have known Cait lived?
Would he have gone through the rest of his days never
even suspecting Allie existed?

Allie said something he couldn't understand, and he
instinctively looked at Cait for translation. Silent tears
were snaking down her cheeks and her lower lip was
caught between her teeth as if holding in a sob. Whatever fist had wrenched that door open dragged it even
wider now, forcing him to be flooded with feelings he'd
locked away two years ago, emotions he hadn't understood then and couldn't begin now.

Cait swiped at her eyes with the heel of her hand. "She
said 'stranger man.'"

Alec couldn't withhold the flinch that erased the unfamiliar grin from his face. He *was* a strange man to
Allie. Stranger Man. It might well be an epitaph for his
entire life. Different cities, names, identities . . . a newly
discovered daughter who called him "stranger."

When he'd been staring dumbfoundedly at the television screen in his cabin in New Mexico, going over the possible reasons for his friends' not telling him about Cait, he'd been puzzled, somewhat angry, yes, but primarily confused, then worried.

Now, seeing Cait's tears, the innocent smile on his newfound daughter's face, he felt a surge of rage like nothing he'd ever encountered.

In New Mexico he'd focused only on the question *Why?* Now all he could wonder was how they *dared* rob him of this. Of Cait. Of Allie.

Perhaps he and Cait wouldn't have made it together, would have drifted apart. He would never know the answer to that one, for those two years could never be retrieved. But he knew to his very soul that no matter what might have happened between him and Cait he would never, *never* have turned his back on Allie, on this tiny living reality of a dream only scarcely begun before it was snatched away from him.

Alec clamped his mind closed on the thought of what Cait had gone through these past two years: no financial support, no husband to turn to in the middle of the night. He didn't dare contemplate these horrors, for a far more tangible and present horror existed at the moment.

He'd been standing gawking at his daughter and her mother as if all of them had aeons of time reeling on endless ribbons in front of them. That wasn't the case at all. And the odds were now tipped dangerously low on their behalf. This afternoon there'd been only himself, an experienced FBI agent, for him to worry about. Once he'd arrived here, he had Cait to take care of. And now, in the predawn hours, there was a family to get to safety. A *family*.

"Cait."

She looked at him, her wariness stronger than ever, her ever-alert antenna raised and quivering at the tone of his voice.

"We have got to get out of here. I'll hold the—Allie—while you get dressed. It would be quicker if you pack for her, you know what she needs."

"Alec, we can't just leave with you." She said it almost casually, as if he were asking her to take a run to the park with him.

"You don't have a choice. I won't take a chance with your lives. I'm sorry I got you into this. But sorry doesn't change the fact that you could be in real trouble if you stay."

He didn't blame her for resisting. In fact, in other circumstances, distrust would have been exactly the right attitude to take. But he had to make her understand her very life was in jeopardy.

"I hate this," she said almost petulantly. "Why can't—?"

"Hell, Cait, if I'm right, what difference does it make? We've got to get out of here!"

"And if you're wrong?"

"I'm not wrong."

"But—"

"If I'm wrong, I'll apologize. I'll...I'll arrange a live-in maid so you can sleep for a month. I don't know anything for sure. But we can't afford to risk it. We've got to get going. Now!"

He turned his eyes meaningfully toward Allie before meeting Cait's agonized gaze again. He hated watching the color ebb from her lovely face. He hated himself for having brought this into her world.

Alec strode across the room and held out his arms for his daughter. Desperate as he was to get a move on, he was nonetheless terrified of having Cait transfer Allie to him. What if he dropped her? What if she cried? What if she hated him?

Cait stared at him wildly, holding Allie as if Alec had a gun trained on her and not merely his outstretched arms. Finally, a visible shudder worked through her and she gently deposited Allie into his arms.

Alec looked down at the little girl and realized he was holding his daughter for the first time. Dazedly, he thought she weighed about the same as his gym bag. But any similarity between the animate and inanimate ended there; she squirmed and wriggled, shifted and turned to find a more comfortable position.

Nervously he jostled her so that she straddled his left hip, unconsciously keeping his right arm free to reach for the gun tucked neatly against his flank. He looked up to see that Cait hadn't moved. She was staring at him as if he'd done something miraculous. She would never know how accurate she was.

He wanted to say something to her, let her know how profoundly holding his daughter for the first time moved him. But some things couldn't be expressed, could only be felt.

"Quickly, Cait. I've got a really bad feeling we're on borrowed time." Even as the words left his mouth, he had the strange sensation that for him, unable to tear his eyes from his daughter, time ceased to hold concrete meaning.

"Alec—?"

He looked up at her. "I'm serious, Cait. Deadly serious." And he was, but part of that seriousness arose from a hitherto unknown consciousness of abject responsibility. This not-so-tiny infant owed her life to him and, as a result of this awareness, he owed her safety, protection.

He ached to tell Cait some of this, but could see, when he looked up, she already knew. That acute sensation of responsibility, of commitment had come to her with her first holding of Allie, probably before that even, and had found a permanent place inside her.

He watched her pause one last time, obviously torn between one duty and another, then she ran from the room, leaving him in the golden light, holding his little dark-haired, blue-eyed baby girl.

The baby—*his daughter*—wrapped a tiny, perfect hand around his thumb and tugged hard. With her other hand she employed remarkably nimble fingers to cling to a handful of shirt with enough strength that Alec suspected she would pull it off before he could pry it free.

She gazed up at him, her candid blue eyes fathomless, adultlike in their appraisal, utterly childlike in their lack of judgment.

He was a *father*. This incredible wonder in his arms was *his* daughter. His.

"Hello, Allie," he said unsteadily.

"Yo-yo," his daughter answered, staring up at him with heart-stopping innocent solemnity.

As a greeting between father and daughter, it might have seemed imperfect, clumsy even, but for Alec a tentative bridge had been flung across a tremendous chasm.

"Yo-yo, little one," he said huskily and stroked a dark curl from her baby-soft brow.

She gurgled something indistinguishable, though her broad wave indicated it could mean anything from the bright mobile above her bed to the butterflies painted on the wall beside her crib. Whatever it was, it seemed to make her happy, and she leaned back in his arms with the flexible back arch that only the totally trusting could manage.

Alec's heart performed a slow and thoroughly painful flip. But the grin that had rested so uncomfortably on his lips earlier felt much more at home now.

"Do you know who I am?" he asked, and this time the hoarseness of his whisper didn't surprise him.

His daughter turned her evening-sky blue eyes on him and stared at him, as if waiting for an answer.

"I'm your—" He stopped, unable to choose between *father* and *daddy,* not feeling he had the right to either title somehow, and not quite understanding why. "I'm here for you."

Cait fumbled with the buttons of her oxford cloth blouse. She'd already had to redo them twice because her fingers were shaking so hard. Her mind was chaos. She could hear Alec's deep voice murmuring something to Allie and heard her daughter's cooing response.

Cait tried telling herself she was only humoring Alec, that whatever danger lurked outside her home existed only in his mind, but she couldn't pretend any longer. She suspected it had been more a feeling of inevitability, the inexorable marching into doom that had wakened her earlier, not any vague noise.

She'd taken only seconds to dress and stuff a handful of assorted clothing into an overnight bag. Out of habit she paused before the full-length mirror on the back of her bedroom door. She stared at her own image. Fear-induced wide eyes, pale face, tousled hair. She looked like a winter shut-in heading out for a weekend in the country.

A two-story house in the country.

She grabbed her overnight bag and rushed out of her bedroom. She stopped midflight, immobilized by the sight of Alec MacLaine holding her daughter in his arms.

It was too much like the dreams that had plagued her for two interminable years.

But in the dreams, Alec would be tickling his baby, bouncing her, making her laugh. In reality, he held Allie somewhat ineptly in the crook of his left arm and the baby's diapered fanny rested on his hip while he separated two slats of the hallway blinds, peering down at the front walkway.

He held Allie unnaturally, as if afraid of her, fearful, perhaps, of dropping her. His grip underscored his absence, his unfamiliarity with his daughter. But not all of the tension in Alec's semisilhouetted form could be attributed to his lack of acquaintance with Allie. When she made some noise and he turned, she could easily read the myriad emotions churning inside him. His lips appeared lined with white, as if he were in pain. A smear of his blood shone wetly on Allie's fuzzy pajamas.

"Ready?" he asked.

"Almost. I just need some things for Allie."

"I—hurry, Cait. And get your coats. It's cold."

She brushed past him, wanting to ask him what he'd been about to say, not daring to think about the incongruity of his presence, but shockingly conscious of his solid reality, his aura filling her hallway, his body radiating magnetic heat.

Her hands trembled again as she thrust disposable diapers, extra clothes, towelettes and a few of Allie's favorite small toys into a second carryall. But this time her hands didn't shake out of fear, but from memory, memory of those three days with Alec seemingly a lifetime ago, and in remembrance of the kiss they'd shared at the base of her stairs only minutes before.

"Oh, damn," he swore from his position at the window.

''What?'' She grabbed the second bag and ran from Allie's bedroom.

Alec's face was a study of despair. He was staring through the parted blind slats, looking for all the world as if his best friend had just been killed in front of him.

''It's Jack,'' he said. His voice sounded hollow and far away. Whoever Jack was, his arrival signified much more than danger: it was a serrated knife thrust in Alec's heart.

Cait waited as Alec drew his fingers from the slats, carefully replacing them to avoid discernible movement. He turned to face her and she felt his pain to her depths. She didn't understand what was happening in this bizarre predawn, hadn't had the opportunity to sort out her feelings about Alec alive, his being there in her home, holding her daughter, but his expression of utter betrayal flayed her raw. She knew what betrayal felt like.

''What do we do now?''

Without hesitation he asked, ''Where's your car?''

''The garage.''

''Attached to the house?''

''Yes. Through the kitchen.''

''Do you have an automatic garage door?''

''Yes.''

''Good. Let's go.'' He hitched Allie more firmly on his hip, his broad hand splayed across her little back, and turned to lead the way down the stairs while Cait raced back for Allie's blanket.

Cait flew down the stairs, pausing only to grab the overnight bag he'd tossed on her floor earlier. She caught up with him in the dining room just as the floodlights on the porch blinked on, shining brightly through the windows flanking the front door.

She froze and instinctively shrank against him. He jerked his head in the direction of the kitchen. She forged ahead of him, her watery legs moving by sheer force of will.

They whisked through the kitchen in absolute silence. Even Allie, as if sensing something extraordinary, tucked her forefinger in her mouth and sucked on it while watching everything with placid curiosity.

Cait whipped her overcoat from the peg just inside the kitchen and, because of her burden with the overnight bags, didn't bother to take the time to put it on.

Just before opening the door that led to the garage, Alec leaned down to whisper in Cait's ear, "Does the garage light come on automatically?"

"No, you have to use a switch."

"Good. Don't touch it. He could see the light come on from where he's standing. Better to let him think you're upstairs."

He lifted a hand to her face and cupped it gently. To her horror, his hand trembled. "It'll be all right," he said. "We'll make it."

"Alec..." She wanted to say something important, something that might bridge the gap between yesteryear and this too frightening morning, suddenly terrified she might lose him again before the shock of finding him had even had a chance to wear off. And she wanted, *needed*, deeper reassurance that all would be well. It wasn't like before; she had Allie to think about, and the concept of something happening to her daughter struck cold, icy terror in every cell of her body.

As if reading her mind, he repeated, "It'll be all right. We'll have to make our way in the dark until the kitchen door is closed and we're to the car. You take the baby. I'll drive. Try to be as quiet as possible until we're actually in the car."

"The keys. My purse. I left them on the counter."

Alec didn't swear at the momentary delay, but he might as well have; Cait could feel his impatience echoed in her own ragged breathing, could feel the seconds pounding in her throat. She snatched the bag from the countertop as the doorbell pealed through the town house. She flew back to Alec, scarcely touching the floor. She skidded into him, grabbed Allie from his arms and hesitated only a split second while he hauled the three pieces of luggage from her shoulders before running into the garage.

This can't be happening. This can't be happening. Like a litany against reality, Cait found herself chanting the words, mouthing them in the darkness.

But it was real. It was happening. To *her.* To them. Her heart felt like a faulty engine piston, chugging too hard, too fast. Each beat punctuated the need for escape. *Hurry...hurry...hurry.* Fear carried her on winged feet. She heard a disembodied voice whispering, *No, no, no,* and was halfway around the car when she realized it was her own desperate denial.

Alec pulled the kitchen door closed and plunged them into abject darkness. She bit back a cry as she stumbled and felt for the hood of her Skylark. She jerked open the back door of the car as Alec did the driver's door. Instantly the interior car lights seemed to flood the garage.

"Oh, God," she muttered, sending puffs of warm air to hang in the cold garage. She thrust Allie into her car seat, forcing her baby arms through the safety harness, silently begging her daughter to be quiet, to be good, to be safe.

"I closed the kitchen door. Jack's alone," Alec said softly. "He's still ringing the doorbell. He can't see the light in here now."

Cait didn't know if Alec was merely informing her of the latest development or had intended to calm her with the reassurance, but it did the trick; her hands stopped shaking long enough to finish securing the harness, cover her daughter with her own coat, lock and shut the rear door and swing into the passenger seat. She closed her door as quietly as she'd just seen Alec shut his.

"Where's your remote for the garage door?" Alec asked softly, if no less urgently. She grabbed the remote from where it was secured to the driver's visor and handed it to him. "Okay. Now put the blanket over Allie. All the way over, understand?"

His cool command served as a catalyst for a wave of pure terror to wash over Cait. She did as he asked without question, horrified at the implication; he was trying to let her know that glass might fly. When she turned back around, Alec had already inserted the key in the ignition and was leaning over to see how many pedals he had to work with on the floor.

"It's an automatic," she said.

He nodded, but still didn't turn the key. Cait envisioned the door from the kitchen bursting open and Jack-whoever to come barreling out at them, guns blazing.

"Are you buckled in?" he asked.

It was such a mundane question it stripped the vision of the insane FBI agent drawing a bead on Alec. The awareness of the reason for his asking steadied her instead of making her even more afraid. Like Allie beneath the blanket, burbling her delight in this new, strange game, Cait was to fasten her belt and lie low to avoid being shot.

Alec knew what he was doing. He was—or had been— a federal agent. Wherever he'd been for two years, he was still a trained professional and she could rely on him to get her and Allie to some port of safety.

"Okay," he said. "I'm going to start the car and then press the remote. As soon as it starts to move, you're going to scrunch down and I'm going to slam the car into Reverse and gun the motor. It'll scream and we'll probably take off part of your garage door and your insurance company'll have a heyday over the ruined paint job to your car. But we'll be out of here," he said. "Now. Are you ready?"

"No," she muttered. No one would be ready for this. No one should be.

"Okay. Here we go."

"Me...me," Allie called out from the back seat, apparently tiring of the blanket game.

"Hush, sweetie," Cait said. "I'm right here."

"Sit tight, Allie," Alec said as he angled around until his right arm rested on the back of the driver's seat and his eyes were on the garage door. "Stanger Man is going to try to save the day."

He turned the key and the car seemed to roar to life. To Cait, the noise was thunderous, deafening, and a dead giveaway of their whereabouts.

Alec reached up without taking his eyes from the double-wide door and depressed the remote. He threw the car into Reverse the very second the big door began rolling up. His right leg jackknifed to grind the accelerator to the floor.

The car leapt backward and lunged toward the painfully slow garage door. With a squeal of tires and a scream of seeming protest, the Skylark slammed into the garage door.

Cait couldn't hold her cry when the garage door scraped against the car roof with a sickening screech. The door, set to spring away from blockage, but prevented from immediate response by the car's impact, wailed its

own groan of protest and ground sideways, wrenching
bolts from stays and shuddering violently across the top
of the car. It jerked to the right a nanosecond before it
would have shattered the windshield.

Alec continued his fierce depression of the accelerator
and the Skylark shot out of the garage and down the
slight incline of Cait's driveway.

"Hold on," Alec said when they reached the street. He
suddenly jerked the emergency brake to an upright position while still jamming his foot on the accelerator. Cait
gripped the seat with frantic desperation as the car tires
screamed and the Skylark skidded sideways, whirling in
a sickening 180-degree turn.

Alec released the emergency brake, if not his pressure
on the floor pedal, and the car leapt forward with a defiant growl that tore up the pavement. Cait thought she
heard someone shouting, but it might have been her own
throaty cries of fear.

Allie giggled in the back seat, blissfully unaware of the
danger, and called out, " 'Gin!"

"What does she want?" Alec yelled, still gunning the
motor to capacity, forcing the car to speed through the
quiet neighborhood as if furious demons were hot in
pursuit.

"She wants to do it again," Cait said weakly.

Alec didn't respond for several seconds, his concentration on their escape. His face was tinted pale green in
the wash of light from the dashboard.

Then, shocking her, stunning her anew on this dawn of
impossible events, Alec chuckled. "That's my girl."

Chapter 7

G-force held Cait pinned to the passenger seat of the speeding Skylark. Her garage door was destroyed, her new car surely needed thousands of dollars worth of repair, and she and her baby were careening through the night with a man she'd seen shot and killed two years before.

She shivered and was certain it had little to do with the temperature. They were heading into who could even guess what further danger, someone within the FBI wanting to kill her—*kill* her—and her stupid brain seemed only capable of focusing on one thing: Alec MacLaine was really alive.

He drove the car through the nearly silent streets of Bethesda at a speed Cait would never have considered even in an emergency situation, but somehow he exuded an air of calm, his skill with the wheel uncanny and sure.

His eyes continually flicked from the street ahead to the rearview mirror as he whisked the car from side street to side street, taking them deeper into a seeming maze of endless sleeping neighborhoods.

Cait recognized Takoma Park, Maryland, then a few sharp turns later realized they'd crossed into D.C. A few cars, driven by tired, slow drivers, scuttled out of the way as Alec forced the car through Adam's Morgan, ritzy Kalorama, down California, up, over and down into the narrow streets of Georgetown.

The normally bustling, jostling pocket of the District noted for specialty boutiques, exclusive restaurants, high-class hospitals and universities was lit by the arc lights that lent the entire city of D.C. a golden glow, making the brick streets glisten as if wet. Like the rest of the world, Georgetown slept, but Cait had the feeling the sleep wasn't easy, and that any moment another car would whip in front of them and the small prestigious section of the District would wake and eat them alive.

Down M Street, and over Key Bridge, then with a final sharp turn, Alec took them onto the George Washington Memorial Parkway. The normally lovely highway seemed ominous now; tall, leafless trees seemed to meet over the top of the car, forming a spiderwebbed tunnel.

Alec had finally slowed the car to a reasonable rate, one still far exceeding the speed limit, but which allowed Cait to check on Allie without being catapulted on top of her. He turned on the heater as she pulled the blanket from the baby's head.

She had to smile, however shakily, at the sight of Allie's sleeping form, her dark lashes shadowing her cheek, her right forefinger imperfectly dangling from her lax lips.

"She okay?" Alec asked.

"Asleep," Cait answered, turning back around.

"Asleep?" He shifted slightly to look at his daughter in the rearview mirror. "I'll be damned."

During the race out of the house, the giddying turns through the city, Cait had clung to the base of her seat, thinking of nothing but escape. Now, on the smooth and empty stretch of predawn, Saturday-morning parkway, she became all too aware of Alec sitting inches from her, close enough she had to shift her knees to avoid brushing his. The Skylark had seemed large when she bought it, spacious enough for her and Allie at any rate. Now it seemed too small, dwarfed by Alec's personality.

They rode silently, neither of them speaking. But the silence wasn't comfortable, the distance between them as distinct and crystal clear as if each day of the missing two years sat in the car with them, every one of them demanding attention.

Stranger Man, as Allie had called him, and he'd repeated, had come back for her. But it wasn't as simple as the words seemed to imply. He hadn't shown up on her doorstep after two years prepared to sweep her into his arms and carry her away into the night, though ironically, he'd done both.

She had no doubts that his fear for her safety was real; the look of stark fear on his otherwise composed features had compelled her to go with him. And she didn't hold any reservations about her safety with *him*. Of all things, she couldn't question that.

In her fantasy, her thousands of dreams about Alec, she'd known for certain that what they had found in that dark closet would have survived for eternity, that they would have endured the trials and tribulations of life in the modern world, the world outside their narrow prison cell. Now she saw how thoroughly she'd bought into her own delusions.

The man who easily sped her car through the night—despite clenched jaw and white knuckles—was the same man who had grinned crookedly at his newly discovered daughter. *This* man, a walking, breathing dichotomy was the reality. A federal agent who had faked his own death. A mystery man. A stranger.

Sneaking a glance at him now, his face reflected in the eerie green light on the windshield, seeing the blue eyes so like Allie's—and yet unlike them, too, for his were focused, driven, haunted, whereas Allie's were guileless, open, trusting—she fought the urge to simply tell him to stop the car and let them out of this nightmare.

But where could she take her baby? Aunt Margaret, certainly, but once there, who could they possibly trust? How would she know that someone else wouldn't come knocking on her door a week from now, a month, a year…carrying a gun packed with bullets marked for her and Allie?

She could only stay where she was, go along with this wild escapade that might save her life, speeding through the night with her one-time lover.

Without turning to look at her, Alec broke the silence that hovered between them like a palpable presence. "I suppose I should tell you that my badge was retired."

She gaped at him. He was cracking a joke?

"I don't even know you, do I?" she slowly asked, interrupting him. "I thought I did, when we were together back then. I thought I knew everything."

"You did," he said. And she heard the sorrow in his voice. The regret.

"No, I didn't even know what you did for a living. Isn't that odd, Alec? We spent three days together. We even made a child together. I suppose, in some cosmic sense, we even died together. And I never asked what you did for a living."

"It didn't seem important then."

Cait felt strangely disconnected, as if they were talking about other people, a time that had happened to someone else. "No. I suppose it didn't."

"I never lied to you, Cait."

She turned her face to the window and stared out at the November darkness. Silhouettes of pale-barked, leafless trees and the flickers of frost on the thick underbrush created the illusion that vast forests stretched on either side of the parkway. But Cait knew it wasn't true; it was only a disguise. Entire cities stretched beyond the black thicket of trees and brush. Whole towns were hidden in the dense Virginia woods.

Like Alec, she thought. Disguises within masks. A lover hidden in the agent, an agent hidden in the man.

"No?" she asked softly.

"I didn't lie, Cait."

So softly she felt him have to lean toward her to hear, she said, "You didn't tell me you were with the FBI. You let me believe you were dead. You let the whole world believe that."

She turned away from her contemplation of the dark forest. He'd straightened and was staring out the windshield with a hard, almost angry concentration.

"I know those weren't lies per se," she added. "But I feel lied to, nonetheless."

He drew a sharp breath and held it. Finally he exhaled it in a low whoosh. Without looking her way he said, "I told you, Cait, I thought you were dead. Nothing on this earth mattered to me after that.''

Cait felt the truth of his words strike her like a blow. Whatever else had happened, this was raw and unvarnished honesty. That it cost him to tell her she didn't doubt; it cost her to hear the vein of deep pain scoring his carefully neutral voice.

She found she'd felt more comfortable with the careening, high-speed escape from her house than she did this brusque, brutal clarification.

In the past two years, especially in the months before Allie was born, she'd found a measure of comfort in believing that Alec would have told her everything sooner or later. She'd told herself they were meant to be together in every sense of the word. In time, in the nurturing environment of the love that surely would have developed, he would have revealed all.

But he'd died. And all revelations had been forced to wait until now.

Nothing on this earth mattered after that.

Not for him, perhaps, but for her, everything that mattered had happened since. Allie's birth, her first tooth, the night her fever rose to 102 degrees and scared Cait half to death. She'd been recognized in a field where many played and few were paid.

Then Cait understood: he could tell her the raw and hurtful truth because it was as buried in the past as he'd thought her. As she'd thought him.

The time for dreams and promises was gone. All the truths and pretty words in the world wouldn't give them back their unique harmony. They were only acquaintances now, people who had known each other once during a stressful time. They might not have been buried in graves somewhere, but the magic had been put in a box and covered up with two years of dirt.

"Caitie—"

Caitie? No one but Alec had ever called her that, and then only once, in the height of a desperate passion. A passion she strongly wished was as buried as the magic and as deeply as she'd thought Alec had been.

"Cait," she corrected, though the memory made her flush with heat, with unresolved emotion. With unfulfilled life.

"Cait. I can't apologize enough."

"I don't want your apologies, Alec." She felt like crying, but tears never seemed so remote. She turned in her seat to face him even though he wasn't looking at her. "I want explanations. I want information. I'm a computer programmer, remember? Give me something I can link together with something else. I need to make some kind of sense out of all this."

What she needed was not to face the painful reality of their shattered beginning. But if they could talk about the mundane, the factual, the nitty-gritty details of how they came to be in this car whizzing through the November predawn, then maybe she could quell the memories of his touch, his taste . . . the feel of his heart pounding against her chest.

"So do I," he muttered, making her wonder if he wasn't thinking along the same lines as she.

"I have a right to know everything. No lies. No half lies. I have a baby in the back seat and I'm . . . scared to death."

He ran a hand through his hair. "God, Cait, I'm sor—"

"Don't apologize, Alec. Just clue me in," she snapped, then, appalled at the sharp silence in the car, added, "I'm sorry. I don't know what made me—"

"I do," he interrupted. "And you have every right to be upset."

After a long, breath-steadying moment, she clearly, carefully said, "Don't patronize me, Alec. Of all things, I don't deserve that."

"You're right. You don't." He stared straight ahead for a seemingly endless time.

She read the signs announcing the parkway's funneling into the beltway and waited until Alec aimed them to the Virginia exit before bringing up the commonplace. "Where are we going?"

His answer wasn't satisfactory. "I don't know yet. We have to get off the beltway soon, then ditch the car."

He said it so casually—*ditch the car.* He didn't know how many months she'd juggled her budget to be able to afford the Skylark. He didn't know how many times she'd driven to the car lot to simply sit in her old battered Ford and covet it. He didn't know about so much.

"Oh, well," she said, as if resigned to the inevitable. "It needs a new paint job now. Might as well get rid of it."

He gave a snort that could have been laughter. She smiled, and was amazed to find she could.

"Was the man who showed up at my house... Jack?... one of your friends?"

"Until this last week, I would have said he's one of the best men I know."

"But something changed your mind."

"Yes."

"What was that?"

Alec looked as if he were staring into the past, not at the highway. "He knew I was there."

"Why do you say that?"

"I heard him calling my name as we left."

"As you demolished my garage."

He smiled and her throat tightened with an ache she couldn't define. She was coming to terms with the simple fact that they were essentially strangers now, so why should the mere sight of his smile make her heart race and tears sting her eyes?

"You said 'until last week.' What happened then? What did you discover, I mean?"

"I came across a document that I was never meant to see. That's how I found out the terrorists that held us hostage were hired by someone in my own division."

Cait digested this rancid revelation. Suddenly the fear the quick repartee had masked was revealed again. "Hired to kill you."

"I think so, yes. At least, that's what the memo said. Until tonight, I had three names. Suspects, if you want. Now I know it was Jack."

"Your good friend."

"My good friend."

"Alec . . . ?"

He glanced at her. His expression was flat, slightly dull, as if he'd been pushed beyond his endurance and was operating on autopilot.

"Who is he? Jack, I mean. I know he's FBI and was your friend, but specifically, who is he and why would he want you dead?"

"Jack King," he said slowly, as if the name burned his tongue. He clicked on the turn signal and edged the car into the left-hand exit lane to Reston, Virginia. "I've known him for fifteen years. We've taken bullets for each other."

"You make it sound like you shared a pizza."

He shot her a look.

She'd deliberately tried to make him smile, to lighten his sense of despair at such a betrayal of fifteen years of friendship. Cait could see that for Alec, knowing his friend was involved was knowing a world of hurt.

Cait sighed with relief when Alec pulled in to one of the huge motel parking lots off Route 7, but her nerves tightened when he told her to stay in the car and wait for him.

"Why?" she asked. "What's going on now?"

"Nothing much. Just sit tight."

"Why?" she repeated.

He flashed her a grin. "We're stealing a car."

Chapter 8

Cait watched in mild horror as Alec crept behind the parked cars belonging to the motel patrons, who slept unaware in their cozy rooms. He knelt at a dust-covered two-door and, using some apparently magic tool extracted from a pocket, removed the license plates from both front and back of the car. Tucking these under one arm, he prowled among the parked vehicles.

Cait slid down in the front seat of the Skylark, torn between reluctant admiration at Alec's resourcefulness and the guilt-by-association surety they'd be caught and hauled into jail, a definitively ignominious coda to the night's activities. While Alec peered in the driver's windows of several other cars, Cait willed every motel door to stay firmly shut, all lights to remain out.

When Alec hunched over and softly pried open the door of a midsize sedan, Cait understood with blinding clarity that if someone did come barreling out of their motel room door, demanding he cease and desist, she wouldn't have the foggiest notion of what to do.

She released her breath only when he shut the door again, but her relief was short-lived; he removed the plates of that car, as well. Before rising from his crouch, he installed the stolen plates on the sedan. With the extra set of plates beneath his arm, he raced back to where Cait was waiting and slid behind the wheel of her car.

"What do you think you're doing?" she whispered sharply.

"Stalling for time," he said. Too calmly. "We can't afford to be traced."

She'd known the trouble was serious, had fled with him in the middle of the night, every instinct a-jangle. But somehow, perhaps still dwelling in that fantasy state she'd lived in for the past two years, she'd falsely assumed that all would be well once they'd abandoned her well-lit house. Her heart beat at a too rapid, too uncomfortable pace, but she didn't say anything as Alec quietly steered the Skylark to an empty slot in front of a motel room and turned the car off.

"Get Allie and take her to the other car. I'll be right with you."

"I'm doing no such thing," Cait said. "You're planning to steal that car and—"

Alec's hand shot out and grabbed her arm, scaring her every bit as much as he'd intended. The man with the chuckle, the acquaintance with the well-remembered smile disappeared. In his place was a determined professional agent.

"Stealing is the very least of our worries right now. Get Allie and strap her in the back seat of the car."

Cait wanted to argue, to whip herself—and him—into that place where anger could take precedence over fear, pain and memories, but she couldn't because he was right. Theft was a mere bagatelle to murder. Her murder.

She opened her mouth to explain, needing to say she was sorry for acting so foolish, but he'd already released her and slipped from the car. Her knees shaking and her hands trembling, she did as he asked, carrying her sleeping daughter in her car seat across the pavement to the car he'd selected for them.

The black-with-a-teal-pinstripe older model sedan was a luxury car with every convenience, including, no doubt, climate control. And the owners had kept it immaculately clean. Her own back seat was littered with bits of cookie, scraps of torn paper and a small collection of abandoned toys, though she'd only been making payments on the vehicle for four months.

She silently vowed to the unknown owners not to damage the car as she strapped the runners of Allie's car seat into place. Once that was done, she quickly and quietly locked and shut the back door before slipping into the front seat to wait for Alec.

In the back seat, Allie sucked in her cheeks and gave a soft mewl that made Cait whirl around to check her—shush her—irrationally afraid the owners of the car might hear this faint baby sound—but Allie quickly settled back into that boneless sleep of the very young.

Alec joined them seconds later, nearly making Cait scream when the interior lights of the car flashed on. A sheen of sweat stood out on his forehead, not from exertion, she thought, but more likely from anxiety and from exposure to the cold predawn air.

He reached for the keys in the ignition and Cait suddenly understood what Alec had been looking for in his window peeking: a car that some owner had carelessly left for them to steal. And the plate switching was to add to the confusion sure to abound when the owner discovered the car missing.

Cait waited for the owners of the car to fly out of the motel. But no lights came on, no one in a robe and slippers screamed at them to stop. They exited the parking lot and took off down the Lee Highway in the direction of Vienna, Reston, Sterling, or historical towns beyond, places Cait couldn't even begin to name right then.

She didn't care where they were going this time; she was too busy feeling relieved they were in a different car. No one would be searching for them in a black sedan with Virginia plates.

She glanced in the back seat at her sleeping daughter. As confusingly in tune with her thoughts as ever, Alec asked, "She's still asleep?"

"Out cold," Cait replied, turning back around.

They drove in silence for several minutes, then Alec cleared his throat. "Are you all right?"

She didn't respond at first. There wasn't any answer but a lie to give him. High-speed chases, guns, people popping back from the grave, stealing cars, those things didn't mix with mortgage payments, diaper bags and cutting teeth. The latter had been the sum total of her past couple of years. The fact that she designed software about the former seemed totally irrelevant.

"Not even close," she answered truthfully, then gave him a measure of reassurance. "But I do feel better in this car. Thanks."

He grinned, but refrained from uttering a deadly I-told-you-so. "No one was following us, and I didn't see anybody link up, so I think we're all right for the time being."

"What happens now?" she asked.

"We hole up somewhere."

"Do you have a plan?"

He flicked her a glance. "Yeah. Not the best, maybe, but a plan."

"Well?"

A flush stained his cheeks. "It doesn't sound like much. Yet. I want to go public with what I've found. Once the press gets wind of this, really gets involved, our chances go up."

"Then shouldn't we go to the authorities?"

"The FBI is pretty high on the authority food chain," he said. "We go to the police, and the FBI will be called in. While I'm busy explaining what I'm doing alive, Jack'll be escorting you into a car. No dice."

"So we call the newspapers."

"And television. I never thought I'd live to see the day I'd be trying to get on the news."

"We just phone them up?"

"And leak pieces of the documents I found."

"Connecting this Jack to the incident two years ago."

"Exactly."

"And what about you?" she asked.

"You don't need to worry about that."

Cait stared at him. "Is that one of those 'Don't worry your pretty head about that, little lady' cracks?"

He glanced at her, a crooked, rather sad smile on his lips. "I didn't mean it that way," he said.

"Then you meant you don't know what'll happen. You could still be in danger."

"But you and Allie will be safe."

His inclusion of Allie, his completely natural way of saying his daughter's name, brought tears to Cait's eyes.

"Cait . . . ?"

"Mmm?"

"Did you really cry for months and months?"

His question sliced cleanly through her heart. Her hands curled into fists in her lap. He couldn't really expect her to talk about something so emotional while they were driving about in a stolen car, with people trying to trace their whereabouts so they could *kill* them. At the same time, she knew she couldn't lie to him.

"Is the daytime sky blue?" she asked. And surprising herself, she smiled, however much it felt bittersweet.

He shot her a quick look. He wasn't smiling at all. "Most of the time," he said slowly.

"Well, there you go."

What she'd intended as a light dodge of his question hung between them, solid, flat, concrete evidence of pain. For she had cried. But with the words out, she now felt she didn't know if she'd cried for the loss of Alec or the loss of the dream they'd created in those three days.

Alec lifted his hand from the wheel of the car and gestured, but didn't speak for several seconds. Then he said, "I didn't know. I wish I'd been there for you."

"Me, too."

"Is it too late for us, Cait?"

She wanted to cry. "I can't answer that, Alec. Maybe because it's too unreal right now. Too soon, maybe."

She sluiced sideways, facing him, needing to see his face, as if by reading his expression she could plumb his thoughts. "What happened to you? What really happened, I mean?"

"One of the bullets nicked a main artery. Luckily for me, it lodged there, acting like a finger in the dike."

"You were shot three times."

"Another shattered my collarbone." He touched the base of his Adam's apple, unconsciously letting Cait know how very close he'd come to never being able to tell this story, how closely the lie had come to proving true. "The doctors tell me a third ripped the living daylights out of my right shoulder ligament. Plus there was the little matter of a skull fracture from Vandever's multiple gun-butt-to-the-head tricks."

She thought about the twenty-one-gun salute at his funeral, the one that made her jump as she stood alongside seeming thousands of armed police. Why hadn't she been able to *feel* his continued existence? Something in her should have known.

So many lies. So many damaging, hurtful lies.

"And you—?" he asked.

"I lived," she said.

He gave the ghost of a smile. "I know that now. But...I heard you screaming, then the two shots...then nothing."

Cait could hear in his rough tone and see by the telltale muscle in his jaw how terribly her screams, the gunshots, had impacted on him, probably as much as seeing the bullets striking him had done to her. She studied his grim face, could tell he'd relived that day every bit as much as she had. Oddly, the realization that he'd been marred by that day steadied her somewhat.

Cait had told no one what she knew about that morning. She'd clung to the "unconscious" story with such tenacity she'd almost come to believe it herself. But Alec wasn't some faceless Senate subcommittee flunky taking a deposition. Nor was he an irritating television reporter. He was the father of her child.

"After they shot you," she told him, "they dragged me out of the room. I was screaming and kicking, trying to break free, to get back to you."

Alec's jaw flexed once, and he brought the car back into the left lane with a white-knuckled hand.

"I was terrified and mad at the same time, do you know what I mean?"

"Yes. Go on."

"They were arguing with each other, but I didn't hear what about. Then the weirdest thing happened. The man holding me held his gun up in the air and fired it twice. Almost right in my ear. That was why I stopped screaming, Alec."

Alec swallowed heavily, then nodded.

"He told the others to think for a second. That the FBI was right outside. Then the man that shot you said, 'We were set up.' The little guy—the one who took us to the bathroom?—he put his gun on the floor and said, 'This wasn't part of the plan. I'm not dying for this shit.'"

"And the other one was still holding you?"

"Yes."

"Is he the one who knocked you out?"

"I was never unconscious, Alec."

"What!"

"He pushed me to the floor against a wall and told me if I knew what was good for me, I'd play dead. And if I didn't get killed, act like I knew nothing."

"But you saw everything, didn't you, Cait?"

"Yes."

"Tell me."

Cait's hands were clenched so tightly in her lap that she couldn't feel them. "The four who had held us hostage put down their guns and stepped away from them. They had their hands up. The front doors burst open and the SWAT team, or whatever it was, ran into the room. A man in a suit followed them. I had my eyes mostly closed and was trying very hard to look like I'd been knocked out or had fainted."

Alec gave her a look that conveyed admiration, but his face was pale and his lips were grimly held together.

"Then the man in the suit told one of the SWAT team guys to look for you. One of them came over to me and felt for my pulse. 'She's alive,' he said. 'But pulse rate is thready.' I swear to God I almost giggled. Sometimes I have nightmares that I did."

"You're lucky you didn't."

"I know. Anyway, the guy moved away from me and after a little while I risked opening my eyes a bit. And when the one who went to find you let out a shout, some of the others ran out to join him. I thought they were going to bring out your dead body. I was almost sick. Then the man in the suit ordered the terrorists killed."

"Just like that? And the men obeyed him?"

"Yes."

"Damn."

"Yeah. Then they fired a few rounds from the terrorists' guns and put them in their hands or near their bodies. Then somebody carried you out in a body bag."

"Cait, do you realize what you're saying?"

"Yes, I'm afraid I do"

"And you've been living with this all this time."

"I was *there,* Alec. I saw it."

"That terrorist did you one hell of a favor, telling you to play dead."

"The biggest. But I've never understood why."

"You weren't part of the original plan. Maybe he thought he'd still manage to walk out of there if he had a living witness. Who knows? We might never find out why."

After a few seconds' pause, he said, "It doesn't make sense."

She stared at him as if he'd just spoken in Japanese. "None of any of this makes sense!"

Alec was frowning. "But logic still has a place—"

"Logic?" she interrupted, grateful to feel anger, for anger burned away all fear, lent strength and could mask her confusion about Alec. "It doesn't make sense that I thought you were dead. It doesn't make sense that the FBI would stage such an elaborate funeral and lie to the whole country! It doesn't make sense that somebody would tell you I died!"

"Or that I wouldn't know you'd gotten pregnant."

"Oh, now there, you're wrong. *That* makes perfect sense. That's probably the only thing that does. You thought I was dead. Most dead women I've heard about don't usually spend nine months gestating in their coffins!"

Cait hadn't realized she'd raised her voice until Alec snorted. She sank back against the passenger seat, shocked at her outburst.

Alec's low, rumbling and utterly infectious chuckle brought her back in a hurry. "I haven't heard about that many, either," he said, grinning broadly.

He'd done that with her two years ago, pushed every button to help her defy fear. But it wasn't working now. She didn't have just herself to worry about; she had Allie. Denial, grasping alternative realities to avoid a situation, even simple delusions were only truly possible when one could be selfish, and the moment Allie had arrived

in the world, selfishness had been tossed out the proverbial window.

Nonetheless, humor served as a mask to fear and could
work to defuse the tension between her and Alec. As long
as it didn't spark the chemistry that seemed to crackle
between them, it would be a worthwhile tool to employ.

"Besides," she said, forcing her tone to a light banter,
"you make it sound like a disease. *Gotten* pregnant. In
fact, the whole way of speaking about pregnancy makes
it sound like something you catch."

But Alec wasn't led away from his subject, nor did he
smile as he said, "I can't believe, though, that I didn't
somehow *feel* I was a father."

This was uncannily like her own reaction to his living,
and allowed her to see both sentiments for what they
were: a sense of misplaced guilt at not having somehow
magically "known" the other was kicking about somewhere in the world.

"I'm still blown away," he said.

"At least this time it's only figuratively."

He chuckled. She found she'd said the words just to
hear that lovely rich rumble. It took her back and at the
same time gave her some material for a possible bridge to
the present. But as she'd feared, the sound of his laugh
made her long to touch him, ache to lay her head against
his chest and feel that low growl vibrate against her
cheek.

"Cait?"

She made some sound, turning her face away from him
so he wouldn't see her rising blush, her raw vulnerability. This night held too many dangerous twists and turns,
and wanting Alec MacLaine seemed the most dangerous
of all.

"Would we have made it, if we'd been together after the debacle two years ago?"

That question had been her constant companion for two years. When she rocked Allie back to sleep in the middle of the night, she'd found herself snared by it. When driving to her Metro stop, it would sneak into the car and plague her.

Would we have made it, if . . . ?

The question held beautiful answers only as long as he hadn't been alive to contradict them. He sat beside her now, asking the one question he should never have had to ask. To Cait, in the uncertainty of the dawn's activities, in light of his very presence, there was only one answer possible.

"We did survive it, Alec. We're alive. We're driving a sleeping baby across state lines in a stolen car, but we both made it out of that closet *alive.*"

"So, where do we go from here?"

Cait didn't know if they were good words or not, but at the moment he spoke them, the first rays of morning light poked over the horizon. She knew exactly what he meant, but she couldn't address the future, *their* future, because in her heart she knew that addressing a future meant giving up the fantasies she'd so carefully nurtured.

She deliberately chose to act as if she misunderstood. "You're driving the stolen car, sweetheart. That decision is entirely yours."

"You're an accessory," he quipped back.

"You make me sound like a purse or a pair of shoes."

"You don't look it."

If he'd been looking at her, the words might have stolen her breath; as it was, she could maintain her light, masking badinage. "I guess they would have a hard time prosecuting you," she said.

He chuckled again. "There's some truth to that."

She found she was grateful that he so easily followed her thinking. She half grinned. "I can see the headlines. Dead Man Steals Salesman's Car."

Alec actually laughed out loud. Cait choked back her own gurgle of hysterical response. For a moment she wondered how she could laugh at such a time, then reflected that it was small wonder that she hadn't succumbed to gales of laughter before. Fear could override all other emotions, but it couldn't be sustained for too terribly long by anyone even moderately healthy. Anger had helped, it had overridden the sharper, deadlier elements. But humor... humor was the gift of the gods.

Whether whistling in the dark or cracking punchy jokes in the dawn light, they were gracefully shrinking the night's fears to a more manageable size. Like the sharp, biting comments in the Skylark earlier, this humor was a bridge between them, an olive branch and a safety net at the same time. It had been this way between them two years ago.

And at that time, the brief bursts of humor and sharp retorts had turned to passion. That memory utterly sobered Cait.

As if reading her thoughts, Alec suggested they pull in to a motel in Sterling, a town only a few miles up the road. Cait pressed against the door, staring out at the frost-covered dawn countryside, not seeing a single white weed stalk or the crystalline bare oaks. All she could see was a paint-spattered drop cloth spread over a king-size bed in a Sterling motel room.

They passed an old mill, a housing development of huge, graceful homes, and the rolling white countryside sparkling in the early light, as alluring as it must have been to the early settlers. And all Cait could think about was that she dared not consider the future. She'd created such a perfect fantasy and had pulled it out so often during the past two years, she struggled to reconcile it with the reality sitting so near her. To accept the man beside her she would have to excise the fantasy. Could she do that? Could she really let the dream go?

With Alec now, soon to stop at a motel, once again in danger, trouble stripping away the veneer society usually could place on emotions, she didn't know what to expect, what to think. They were strangers, yet not. She knew everything about him and, truthfully, nothing at all.

Even as she wondered how they are going to get out of their present difficulties, she questioned how much she really wanted out. Terrifying as the night had been, she felt alive. Deeply, acutely *alive.* As vital and on edge as she'd felt in that damnable closet two years before.

Weren't those three days with Alec the most important days of her life? Danger surrounding them, they'd seized life and passion with every fiber of their beings, defiantly spitting at death. And now that danger was back and again she felt stretched beyond the normal limits.

But, another part of her argued, those days were simply days, and days in the dim past. Danger was a peculiar bedfellow, distorting the mind and one's sense of proportion. The important days of her life weren't found in that utility closet two years ago, they were such days as the morning Allie was born, the day her daughter imperfectly said ''Mama'' for the first time. Allie's first words, her first faltering steps, the first day at nursery school. The latest cute thing she did or said.

All those little, extremely vital moments made up the important days, the ones that forged a real, full existence. No matter how lonely she may have felt during the wakeful, darkest hours of the night, no matter how pale those days might seem in contrast with dramatic exits, twenty-one-gun-saluted fallen heroes, and bad guys lurking out there in the dawn, the calm and peaceful days were the meaningful ones.

Alec glanced over at Cait's still form. One minute she'd been wielding a bright rapier of humor, deftly fencing, fighting fear and skewering the past. Yet at the mention of stopping at a motel, she'd laid her point to the floor and bowed out of the game.

If she didn't look so terminally serious, he could point out that he hadn't slept in nearly twenty-four hours, and was probably far more terrified of being alone with her than she could possibly be of him. It wasn't *her* so-called friends trying to kill her.

And she was trusting him to do the right thing by her and Allie, to protect them, to get them out of this mess somehow. He was so damned tired he couldn't think straight. He'd had too many curves thrown at him in the past six hours.

His best friend had lied to him, was likely a traitor to everything Alec believed in.

Cait was alive.

He had a daughter. A beautiful, trusting daughter.

And the three of them were in big, *big* trouble.

He wanted to tell Cait he'd been in plenty of tight spots before and managed to squeak through. But like not telling her about his involvement with the FBI during those days under terrorist seizure, what would be the point of discussing the past now?

This situation was entirely different. On a mission he usually had someone covering his back, or at least faith in a person he could call when the going got too rough. But he wasn't on a mission now. He was embroiled in one. With a woman and baby riding shotgun.

He sifted through the kaleidoscope of emotions roiling in him. Disbelief, anger, outrage, joy, tension . . . the list seemed endless. The only feeling he could identify with any surety was fear. He'd been nervous, even scared, more times than he cared to remember. But he'd never experienced the kind of sinking, heart-jolting terror that flash-fired through him every time his mind skittered across the notion of something happening to Cait or Allie.

Hell, he'd only just found Cait again. And several times in the course of their headlong dash through the dark streets of the city she'd looked at him as though *he* were the bad guy. As if he were a stranger. And his daughter, the baby he'd discovered just that night, called him Stranger Man. Both those discoveries were monumental and frightening in and of themselves, but to compound the enormity of the situation, someone—one of his closest friends—was undoubtedly looking for them right now.

His hands gripped the steering wheel so fiercely that he had to force himself to relax them before he lost feeling. He flicked a look in her direction, suddenly, irrationally angry with her silence. It wasn't his fault that she'd thought him dead; he'd thought the same thing of her. And it wasn't his fault that someone within his own division had apparently lost his marbles.

But she looked so pale, so fragile in the wan light of dawn.

He raised his eyes to the rearview mirror and inched upward a bit to see his daughter sleep. Like a cloth doll, her body draped in total abandon over the side of the car seat. One arm stretched above her head, almost to the top of the headrest, while her curly dark head lolled on the other. Her chubby legs splayed through the harness and seat support in what appeared the most appallingly uncomfortable position, yet a slight smile curved her full lips.

Fourteen months old. Did babies that age walk already? He didn't know, and a wave of despair shook him. He should know. He should have been there to see. His daughter obviously talked a little, even if he needed Cait as a translator. And he should be able to understand her as well because he should have been around long enough to be able to wade through the lisping, unusual sounds that comprised her baby language.

God, he had a daughter. The natural result of an unnatural captivity, the human reward granted after despair and pain. Had Cait hated him for dying? Had she cursed him for not being there for her? He thought of the many times he'd been angry with her for dying on him.

And thought of the confused feelings he now had for Jack King. For it was Jack who had shown up at Cait's house earlier that morning. It was Jack who had obliquely lied to him about Cait dying. But every instinct told him it hadn't been Jack who had ordered the hit on the WHO two years before. What, then, had Jack been after at Cait's?

Cait sighed heavily and he felt his heart twist as she raised one hand to brush the hair from her forehead. Her hair stuck up in little blond spikes and her green eyes were lined with shadows and creased with worry. She stared at the cold, dawn-brightened countryside leading into Ster-

ling as if it were the driest desert in an alien terrain. Her
eyes were bleak, disbelieving.

And she was so damned beautiful. Her features weren't
the classic, sock-you-in-the-stomach gorgeous. There was
far more to Cait than a perfectly oval face, wide-set eyes
and set of pouty lips, though he was sure she had all those
attributes. What he liked best about her looks was that
she seemed a study in contradictions, pixielike turned-up
nose with a splash of freckles across the bridge that
perched over a mouth that would have made Helen of
Troy envious. And a voice that would lure the most
hardened woman hater from his soapbox. She was slight
but had full, rich curves that molded to a man's in perfect symmetry.

He felt short of breath and slightly dizzy.

He'd been a fool to ask Cait where they were going
from there. She couldn't guess any more than he could.
The past was dead, more dead than ever Cait had been.
He understood now that what had been stolen from
them—the dreams, hopes, even the reliability of memory—were gone forever.

They had only now. And the present itself was muta-
ble, fraught with danger. The responsibility for their
safety rested squarely on his shoulders. He had to get
them to safety.

Alec understood Cait's sudden leap into silence. Humor could only stay reality for so long. And the reality
was too grim to allow laughter.

Chapter 9

The motel room wasn't a bit like the torrid picture in Cait's mind. It was large, as motel rooms went, containing two double beds, a table with two chairs, a large cabinet hiding a television and beneath that a chest of drawers.

Inspecting it, she found the room swung left at a vanity sink and mirror with a small dressing alcove leading to a fairly spacious bathroom. Seascapes, the kind found in a million motel rooms across the country, adorned the walls. Cait supposed they were meant to be soothing; instead they made her feel lonely, as turbulent as the seas that churned forever on the inexpensive canvases.

No paint-and-blood-spattered drop cloth draped over either of the double beds, no hint of ammonia perfumed the air. It was simply a motel room, banal in its function, a place to eat and sleep while traveling the highways of America.

The red digital readout on the alarm clock said the day was approaching six-thirty in the morning, and something about seeing the clock, so like her own left behind at home, struck her as incongruous.

This can't be happening.

But her denial only stretched so far. It *was* happening.

She watched as Alec carried the car seat with the still-sleeping Allie into the room. He stood just inside the doorway waiting for her to tell him where—and probably *how*—to settle his daughter.

She gestured to the aisle created by the space between the two beds. In the old days, she thought, parents had used a bolster to separate unmarried couples in bed. A two-foot gap of floor space and a sleeping baby would surely have an even stronger effect.

He deposited Allie and lingered, his hands hovering over her.

"If you try to rearrange her, she'll wake up," Cait said.

"But she looks so uncomfortable," he whispered.

"You don't have to be quiet," she returned. "Aunt Margaret convinced me early on that lots of noise during nap time was a mother's best companion."

He pushed to his feet. He didn't look at her, but Cait could feel his uneasiness from where she stood. They had been so much to each other those three days so long ago, and now they could scarcely talk.

"I've got to get some sleep," Alec announced and, punctuating his statement, yawned hugely.

"And we have to take care of your arm," Cait responded.

He shrugged out of his jacket and then out of the shoulder straps molding his holster to his back.

"Isn't that uncomfortable?" she asked.

"What, this?" he asked, holding up the gun. "Sure, but there's more than one kind of discomfort."

He glanced around the room, studied Allie for a moment, then set the gun, holster and all, on top of the tall television cabinet. His shirt was stained with blood, but it didn't look wet. "If you're hungry, we can call room service," he said. He picked up a menu from the desk and handed it to her.

"Want me to bandage your arm for you?" she asked.

Rolling up his sleeve, he studied his arm. "Looks worse than it is," he replied.

Cait was again struck by how natural the situation could appear, but how dreadfully awkward it was in reality. Mother, father and baby, pulling in to a motel from a hard morning escaping from bad guys and stealing cars. *Order some croissants and coffee, will you, hon? Oh, and a side order of bullets.*

"I'm fine," she said.

He turned and looked at her. "Yes," he said, disconcerting her, making her feel the room was too warm, too small.

He slowly unbuttoned his shirt, his eyes still linked with hers. He tugged the tails from his trousers and unfastened the buttons at his wrists. Cait's mouth went completely dry. A warm rush of purely physical reaction swept over her, swiftly followed by a stab of anger.

How dare he mock her? They were strangers now. Whatever they had shared two years ago, whatever might have produced that sleeping baby, whatever magic that had been had died back then.

Alec continued to meet her gaze—challengingly? Hopefully? Certainly inscrutably. Then he turned aside, his own tension given away by his studied indifference.

"All the same, I think I could use something. Some kind of breakfast, I mean. I don't care what you order."

Cait crossed to the telephone, suddenly feeling the effects of the strange morning. She felt tired in a manner far beyond mere weariness, more a fatigue of the soul. When she'd thought Alec had died, she'd railed against fate for leaving her alone. She thought now that fate had been far more cruel than simple abandonment.

At least alone, she'd felt at ease with the memory of him. Together in this motel room, too aware of him standing within touching distance, hearing the rustle of his shirt, catching a faint whiff of his male scent, she couldn't think of how to do something as simple as just talk with him. Each word carried too much weight, too much meaning. Layers upon layers of nuances hung between them like swords waiting to fall at the slightest unwary statement, ready to slice them apart.

She ordered the motel restaurant's breakfast special of eggs, bacon, fresh fruit, juice, muffins and a pot of coffee with extra cream. When she woke, Allie would be able to eat heartily from the leftovers.

She replaced the receiver and turned around.

In the soft glow of the lamplight, and without his shirt, she thought Alec looked like an advertisement for men's cologne: classic profile of rugged features, dark hair curling at the nape of his neck, broad, muscled shoulders flaring wide over a muscled chest and a rock-hard torso.

But as he turned from his overnight bag, Cait could see the scars that marred the muscled shoulders and drove bolts of pale lightning across his chest, shoulders and sides. And she remembered how the bullets that had formed some of them had slammed him back against the wall of the closet. Each mark on his beautiful body was a grim reminder of how close he'd come to truly dying, the scars a collection of near misses.

Her hands shook in primal, elemental need to touch those scars, brush her fingers against his warm skin, to test her memory, to see if he felt as velvet hot as she remembered.

Alec used a washcloth to remove the blood from his arm, then tugged a fleecy sweatshirt over his head and turned to face Cait. Involuntarily, he checked when he saw her expression. In all his life he'd never known someone so easy to read, so starkly honest with herself, with the world. His heart began to pound in harsh, thunderous rhythm.

Her full lips were parted, her eyes dazed, confused. Her cheeks were stained with color and her breathing was shallow and light. This was no foray down memory lane. She was reacting to him now. Here. In the very real present.

The desire he could see smoldering in her ignited a flame in him, as well. He wanted her. More than he'd ever wanted anything before, except perhaps for moments too strongly remembered from two years ago. And it had been Cait then, too. Was that the secret? If they only gave in, succumbed to that remarkable chemistry that still flared so naturally between them, would the rest follow—the trust, the faith, the acceptance of each other? Was that even possible?

Somehow, without being aware of it, he'd moved closer to her. All he had to do was lift his hand and he could touch her. "Cait..."

She dragged her gaze from his chest and looked up to meet his eyes, a spark of fear flickering in the dazed flame already burning.

He couldn't bear to see her confusion, the longing mingled with doubt, the uncertainty warring with memory. He cupped her silky cheek with his hand. Against her warm face, his fingers felt cold and trembled slightly.

He wanted to hold her against him, remember how she felt and discover her again. He wanted to taste her and to linger there for a thousand years. But he did none of these things, only lightly stroked her face and said her name.

She closed her eyes and frowned slightly, as if in pain. And he knew she was hurting, knew it was the same torture he felt. Closing his own eyes, he used his thumb to trace the delicate planes of her face, remembering, memorizing anew.

He heard her breathing catch, then resume, could feel the thready beat of her heart through his fingertips. He opened his eyes to see her, to watch her reaction to his touch, and found her staring directly at him.

"You're tired," she said hoarsely.

"Yes," he lied, agreeing with her but not moving away, not dropping his hand.

"You need sleep," she said. With relief? Regret?

"Yes."

She lifted her hands, either to draw him close or push him away. She dropped them back to her sides.

"Two years is a long time," she said, her words flaying him raw, and her sad tone poured salt in the wound.

"Yes."

All he would have to do was lower his lips the merest inch. His entire body shook with the need to taste her.

"You're going to kiss me." It wasn't a question but rather a simple acknowledgment of inevitability.

"Yes," he said, not feeling a stitch of inevitability about it. He felt as if he moved against an incoming tide, the tension between them was so strong. He both needed to kiss her and wished himself any other place on earth. Then his lips met hers and the battle was over.

Except for his lips, and the hand on her face, their bodies didn't meet. He forced himself to remain still, not to allow his other hand to rise to her shoulders to draw her into an embrace, although he wanted to, craved doing just that. He didn't run his fingers through her hair or pull her against him to let her know the extent of his want for her.

He only kissed her. Slowly, achingly sweetly. Poignantly. It was both a singular farewell to the past and acknowledgment of the present, the very real *now*. For Alec, and he suspected for Cait as well, the entire world shrank to a single point of contact, a universe of emotion expressed in a single velvet meeting of lips. He knew that apology and regret flavored his caress, while he could taste the bittersweet tang of long-ago tears that salted hers. Their breath mingled and combined as they mutually sampled the curious present, contrasting it with the almost equally strange past.

The kiss—long, exploratory, question and unspoken answer—felt both a blueprint of some possible future and a torch that burned the bridges that linked them in the past. It tasted of reunion and a sad goodbye to the two years they'd lost. And it was a single, thin rope tossed across the two-year chasm that yawned between them, a first hope of a tenuous bridge to the absolute present.

When she drew away from him he had to fight every instinct not to pull her back. He knew if he touched her at that moment, or she him, there would be no holding back, that all barriers and safeguards would crumble. Part of him wanted that collapse, while another part of him struggled to remember the uncertain future, the awkward, nebulous present.

A knock at the door thankfully intruded at the moment of having to face the present, and acted like an icy shower on Alec. He whipped around, grabbed the gun from the top of the cabinet and peered out the spy hole.

He turned with a relieved grin for Cait. "It's a crib I asked them to send round for Allie."

Cait's face had drained of color and she'd dropped to crouch over Allie. Now she shakily pushed to her feet, color returning to her face, her eyes too wide and on the gun he held in his hand.

He shoved the .45 back on top of the cabinet and opened the door for the maid. After he tipped her, he let Cait close and lock the door while he tried opening the crib. He tugged at the supports from various nonfunctional points. "How does this damned thing work?"

She took it from him, depressed raised knobs on either side and popped the bed into shape. She locked the braces, pulled the safety guards over the locks and flipped the mattress into place.

"I'm not going to even ask how you did that," he said, taking the now cumbersome square from her. "Where should I put it?"

Cait was again struck by their almost natural slippage into a sense of being a cohesive team. He'd thought of a crib; she could set it up. He carried it for her, ready to place it where she dictated. Somehow their unity, the sense of being a couple, a pair, felt too easy and its very natural quality made her uncomfortable.

"I don't—in the alcove?"

He disappeared around the corner and came back empty-handed. "Will she wake if you move her into the bed?"

Cait didn't think Allie would wake at anything less than Alec's gun going off, but he'd gone to the trouble of arranging the crib, and he obviously wasn't familiar with a toddler's ability to sleep anywhere, anytime, in any wild position.

"She will, but she'll go right back down as soon as her head touches the mattress. Would you get her blanket for me?"

She wished she could snatch the words back; innocuous as they were, they seemed to underscore that familial, married-couple feeling. And that, more than anything else, seemed to taunt her for her fantasies, her grief, even her careful, well-ordered life.

She wriggled Allie from the car seat harness and ignored the grunts of protest as she lifted the still-sleeping baby into her arms. Alec had stripped the cases from two of the pillows on the beds, but instead of moving to the alcove, he stared at her, at the mildly squirming Allie in her arms, as if he'd never seen a mother and child before.

"She's so beautiful, Cait."

Cait couldn't help the smile of maternal pride that curved her lips.

"So are you," he said.

She could only gaze at him, robbed of speech, cheated now of that very unity she'd felt misgivings about only seconds earlier. His three little words, *so are you,* made her realize now that the sense of being a couple hadn't been truly uncomfortable at all; it had held the threads of passion at bay, had stayed the tension that played between them like an out-of-tune violin, tension that made every nerve ending jangle and every thought become jagged edged with confusion.

She couldn't have moved if her life had depended on it and was exceedingly grateful when he calmly, prosaically preceded her to the alcove and put sheets on the crib's mattress.

She gently deposited their daughter down in the cozy bed. The thought—*their* daughter—caught her unawares and wrenched painfully deep inside her, and more grievously still when he draped Allie's blanket over her pajama-clad back.

He straightened slowly and met Cait's eyes. Again something seemed to pass between them, but like before, she didn't understand the meaning. Then, at the sudden acceleration of her heartbeat, and the warm, blood-rushing sensation of falling, she knew she hadn't wanted to understand; it was far easier to deny than to accept the truth.

And the truth was simple, however devastating. Whatever it was that lay between them, be it past or bonds or even fantasy, there was *some*thing and it burned in him every bit as she could feel it searing her.

Unconsciously, maybe still trying to escape the need she felt threatening to consume her, she backed out of the alcove. But not far enough, not swiftly enough, perhaps purposefully slow.

The moment, like her mind and body, seemed arrested in time, crystallized by conflicting wants and needs. Alec's blue eyes, heavily hooded and slightly red from lack of sleep and worry, gave nothing of his thoughts away, but she could feel his want.

She ached to raise her hand to his cheek, to feel the muscle sure to be flexing there. She fought against his magnetic pull, though he didn't so much as twitch a finger in her direction.

She'd remembered every nuance of their time together, each word, all touches, sounds and smells, but snared by him now, caught in that timeless moment in a motel she couldn't even name, she stared into the present, knowing this impression, this mutual want would override images from the past. This Alec, this man who gazed at her with equal portions of longing and uncertainty, as aware of the fragility of their tenuous present as she could ever be, once had meant the world to her.

And no matter what she'd said, what she'd tried to make herself believe, he wasn't a stranger. He could never be one. They were bound in ways both mysterious and mundane.

A second knock at the door caused Alec to brush past her and again pull the gun from the cabinet before peering out the peephole. The very ease of his action underscored the danger that lurked outside somewhere, danger that threatened them all.

He tucked the gun behind his back in the waistband of his trousers before opening the door to take their breakfast. What was she doing here with a man who carried a gun to answer the door?

Surviving. That's what she was doing. Just trying to survive.

"Maybe the coffee will clear my head," she heard him mutter.

"I don't think it'll help," she murmured, thinking of herself, remembering their kiss.

"No," he agreed. His eyes met hers. "I can only think of one thing that would help."

Her breath caught. This was too fast, too nebulous. Too dangerous.

He turned away. "You must have been reading my mind when you ordered this," he said, lifting the lids off plates and setting them aside. He flashed a grin at her. She smiled weakly back.

He pulled back a chair for her and waited until she was seated before sitting down himself. "Okay, breakfast first, then we'll brainstorm," he said.

Her entire mind was a storm.

"Between the two of us, we should be able to come up with a way to get the whole cover-up out in the open without getting me killed in the process."

"And maybe we can save the Western world while we're at it," she said. If only she could come through this relatively sane.

"Why not?"

"Why not."

Cait buttered the toast; Alec divided the bacon. She added cream to her coffee; he held out his cup for a dollop. She bit into a slice of apple and he said, "It's weird."

She thought he might be reading her thoughts again.

"Being here together like this, I mean. It's like we've never been apart."

Cait couldn't answer, because this time, even if he wasn't conscious of it, she knew he was lying through his teeth. They had never been together in any way except passion. They had shared a few crumbs of meals two years before, but everything had been seasoned with fear, flavored with the knowledge they would soon be killed.

The food now suddenly tasted like cardboard, as empty as the uncertain future.

Instead of designing an ingenious plan to catch the bad guys, as Alec persisted in calling them—finding it easier to refer to them by that casual designation, Cait supposed, than labeling them "friends"—Alec yawned through breakfast and continually eyed the bed closest to the table.

Finally Cait couldn't stand it any longer. "Go to bed, Alec," she ordered. "You said yourself that we're probably safe for the time being. Get some sleep."

When he looked as if he might argue with her, she continued, "We need you alert, thinking." We need you *alive,* she thought. "And you haven't slept since when, yesterday?"

"I dunno," he said, but he rose obediently and headed the two short steps to the bed closest to the door, the vulnerable side of the room. He didn't look at her as he pulled back the covers and removed the gun from the back of his pants. He set it on the nightstand on the left of the bed. After unzipping and removing his trousers, he sat on the edge of the bed and stripped the sweatshirt from his torso, pitching both it and his pants to the chair he'd abandoned. He hiked one leg up to remove his socks seemingly unaware that she sat only a few feet away, her eyes riveted on him, her mouth dry, her heart pounding far too rapidly.

Cait, watching him, again felt that stab of almost casual intimacy. He removed his right sock first, then his left and, instinctively, she knew he always performed the action this way. She didn't remember his removing his socks two years ago. There hadn't been time or need for such a small luxury. The sight of the simple preparation for sleep brought tears to her eyes; she should have seen him do this a thousand times.

Already half asleep, he leaned back against the pillows, releasing a sharp groan of relief or pain. His nearly nude body beckoned her, but she remained in her chair, fingers curled around the wooden arms, nails pressing into the pine. She felt a million cold-hot miles away, watching as he flipped the sheets over him. He sighed roughly.

So did she.

"Aren't you going to sleep?" he asked blurrily. His eyes were already closed, his breathing growing deeper.

"I'm all right," she said, pushing out of her chair and retrieving the gun from the nightstand. She held it gingerly between thumb and forefinger. She didn't look at him as she crossed to the television cabinet and stood on tiptoe, using her fingertip to push the gun on top. She hated it. She hated the need for it. And, irrationally, welcomed its presence as long as Alec held it in his hands.

"I dreamed about you," he murmured.

She froze for a moment, then turned around. His eyes were closed and his mouth lax.

"Me, too," she breathed. "About you."

"You're there every night, Cait. Every damned night."

She felt as if a hot poker were laid against her heart.

"What?"

"What—?" His eyes flickered and opened. "Did I fall asleep? Sorry."

"S'okay," she murmured soothingly, though her head felt light and her hands numb. "Go on to sleep."

"My gun's on the table...."

"I put it on the cabinet," she said.

"That's good. Jack won't think to look there."

"No," Cait whispered, knowing he wasn't really with her, that he'd already crossed over into sleep.

"Bastard," he said.

"Sh-h-h."

"How could you let me think she died?"

"Sh-h-h."

"But she sleeps with me, Jack. She's with me all the time."

Cait, choked by his words, hearing a truth he would never in a million years admit, realized he was far more tired than he'd let on. He'd only said he needed sleep, he hadn't said he was desperate for it, that it would have overtaken him by force if he hadn't lain down.

"You better not," he muttered, turning his head on the pillow restlessly.

"I won't let anything bad happen," she said.

"Oh, good," he said, as if his conscious mind only needed that reassurance before letting go.

"I'm right here," she murmured, unexpected tears blurring his sleeping form.

"Right . . . here," he repeated, his words slurred.

"Good night, Alec."

"Caitie . . ." he mumbled. "Come back to me, Caitie. . . ."

The tears stinging her eyes burned free and spilled down her cheeks.

Chapter 10

Saturday, November 10, 10:30 a.m. EST

"*G*ive her up, Alec."

"Never."

"I'd rather not have to kill you...."

"To get to Cait, you're going to have to."

Jack raised the 9 mm assault rifle in his hands and trained it on his former partner. "Why don't you let it go, Alec? You're only creating problems by protecting her."

"Why did you lie to me, Jack?"

"Get out of the way, Alec."

Something brushed his face; he didn't dare look away from Jack to see what it might be.

"Did you know about the baby?" Alec asked, his eyes on the gun.

Jack started to laugh, and raised the rifle another notch. Alec could see straight down the barrel.

"I warned you, Alec. You can't say I didn't warn you."

Alec swung his arm at the same moment Jack depressed the trigger.

In the split second before he struck, Alec analyzed the touch on his face. He froze in the very act of slamming his fist against Jack's gun, understanding in that nanosecond that he was asleep, dreaming, that there was no gun, no Jack. His eyes flew open to see a wide-eyed, curly-haired infant whose head barely topped the side of the bed.

Allie gazed at his upraised, deadly hand. "Big," she said, her mouth slack with awe.

"Oh, God," he muttered over the huge lump in his throat. He forced his hand to his suddenly cold body. "You'll never know, sweetheart."

Allie said something that sounded like "mameep" and gave him a clue to her meaning by pointing beyond him.

Alec rolled over to see Cait curled on the other bed, facing away from him and obviously deeply asleep. Mameep...Mama is asleep. Baby talk, he realized, wasn't simply mispronounced English. Allie seemed to employ an entirely new variation of the language altogether.

"How did you get out of your bed?" he asked.

"Aleet."

Alec struggled for translation. "What?"

Allie apparently decided he was deaf and repeated the word at a slightly higher volume, then echoed it even louder.

At the third shouting of the incomprehensible word, Alec sat up, disoriented, dry mouthed, thoroughly rattled by the need to provide his overtly distressed daughter with whatever aleet might be.

"I don't understand," he said honestly, earnestly. And abashedly. This was his own daughter, for heaven's sake;

surely it didn't take an advanced degree in linguistics to communicate with a fourteen-month-old baby. People, even a few remarkably stupid people, managed it all the time.

All, apparently, except him. Because he hadn't known she existed, because he hadn't lived with her, grown with her.

"Aleet! Aleet!" Allie yelled with enough lung power to drown a five-alarm pealing bell.

"Hey, hey, hey!" he countered. "I can hear you fine, sweetheart. I just don't understand."

He tried his best grin, the one that invariably made old ladies offer him their seat on the subway, the one that had made him the object of several stray dogs' undying loyalty. It had zero effect on his daughter.

"Aleet!"

"Give me a clue," he said, feeling desperate.

She pounded the bed with baby fists and tears sprang to her enormous blue eyes, filling them, smiting him. As scared of her as he was—and on a fear scale of one to ten, this two-foot-tall baby human registered a full ten—he couldn't let her stand there in overtly abject misery. He reached out and plucked her up from the side of the bed and onto his lap. "Don't cry, honey. Whoa, whoa. I didn't mean to make you cry. I just don't understand."

Huge tears clung to her incredibly long, dark lashes. Her blue eyes, a richer blue than his own, were awash with liquid, brightening them. His heart constricted. Painfully.

"Please," he said. "I want to help you. Just tell me what you want."

She blinked at him, then said slowly, clearly, "Aleet." She stared directly at him, as if she thought him not only deaf but mentally handicapped, as well. She put her hands on either side of his face as if tactile assistance would help him glean her meaning. "Aleet."

Beneath her baby fingers, he repeated her unusual word. She looked startled and her tears stopped as if someone had simply turned them off. He raised his eyebrows. She lifted a finger to touch one.

"Eyes," she said.

"Eye*brows*," he corrected with a crooked smile. His heart pounded furiously. This was his daughter talking to him, his little girl tracing the line of his eyebrow. They were actually communicating. He raised and lowered his eyebrows several times and her baby finger moved with them.

Allie giggled and his heart turned right over. Permanently. Irretrievably and forever hers.

"Eyebrow," he said, and waggled them again just to hear Allie giggle. He felt both inept and wonderful at the same time.

"Trow," she said, making one rise by pushing it herself.

"Good girl. You got it. Eye-brow," Alec said slowly, grinning down at her, lifting and lowering her finger with his shaggy brows.

"Eye," she said, and poked him smack in one.

He couldn't restrain the slight yipe of protest, but it only made her giggle.

"Eye," she said again, digging in.

"Yes, eye." He grimaced, gently prying the offending finger from the now profusely tearing object of her interest. "And you're probably right. I didn't need that one. I have another." Without much luck, he willed the pain to back off and the tears to subside.

He heard a low, throaty chuckle. "Are you all right?"

"Eyes," his daughter said, struggling to free her hand from his grasp so she could undoubtedly press her point.

"Blind in one eye, but otherwise fine," Alec offered, fending off his determined daughter's fingers.

"She was trying to tell you she was hungry."

"That's what that word was?" he asked, risking opening the poked eye. Tears spilled down one cheek. He turned to see a blurred Cait sitting up on her bed. He squeezed the hurt eye shut, unwilling to stop looking at her, however single-focused.

Her short hair was mussed, spiky again. She looked rakish, ready to tackle the world. At the same time he sensed a caution in her, a wariness that made him immediately aware of their unusual circumstances. A small, bittersweet smile played on her lips as she looked at her daughter, but she wouldn't meet his gaze.

She swung her legs over the edge of her bed in a fluid, graceful motion. Her feet arched naturally and for some odd reason the sight stirred him.

She said, "Allie . . . eat."

Alec groaned. "Al eat. Two words. I get it now."

"Aleet, Aleet," Allie said happily, squirming to get free of his restraining arms.

"Well, of course you want to eat," he said, then turned to Cait. "It's going to take me a while."

Cait didn't say anything to that, though her refusal to look at him and her expressive face spoke volumes. Alec wished he could snatch the words back into his mouth. At the very least they implied a future interaction as if bit by bit, slowly but steadily, he would learn to understand his daughter. And nothing Cait had said or done could possibly lead him to believe that time was something she might offer him.

At the most, his words underscored the very real possibility that time was something she didn't even have to offer. Because the plan he'd concocted on the road that morning seemed utterly futile when he stared at her lovely face. Unless he made like a magician and pulled a miracle from his nonexistent magic hat, one of his friends was going to find them.

Cait took Allie from his arms, and while a part of him was relieved—he didn't have a clue how to go about feeding his daughter—another part of him keenly felt the loss of that small bundle of warmth, eye-prodding fingers and all.

"She needs changing," Cait said, swinging a giggling Allie into the air and flopping her down onto the other bed.

Alec wondered how long it had taken Cait to feel that natural with Allie. He was practically dripping with sweat just from the few minutes of holding her, sure in some deep recess of his mind that he'd inadvertently crush her. And Cait casually, even laughingly, flipped her in the air and let go. He didn't think he'd ever be able to do that trick. He felt queasy just trying to imagine it.

While Cait was busy changing Allie, he slid to the edge of the bed and reached for the sweatshirt he couldn't even remember removing. It was neatly folded atop his equally smoothed pants, and his socks were folded across his loafers. A glance at the top of the television cabinet proved that sometime between sitting at the table and waking up to his daughter's delicate touch, his gun had also been restored to its place of safety.

And he knew full well that he hadn't done any of those things.

He must have done a regular striptease for her, though he couldn't remember anything beyond finishing breakfast. Great, MacLaine, he thought. Give the literal woman of your dreams a heart attack by showing up on her doorstep when she thinks you're dead, rush her and her baby that you didn't even know about out of the house, let her be sure to understand someone's trying to kill her and then pass out on her. Smooth.

He dragged his sweatshirt over his head and his pants up his legs. And he couldn't look at Cait when she rounded the bed carrying a happily chattering, wholly incomprehensible Allie to the table.

"How did she get out of that crib?" he asked. "Did she climb out?"

Cait chuckled. "No. She woke up earlier and I got her out. She was willing to be quiet as long as I lay down with her."

Alec didn't know why the words tugged at his heart. Nor did he want to analyze why the notion of lying down with Cait should make his loins suddenly ache.

"Here you go, sweetie," Cait said, depositing Allie in one of the chairs.

Alec thought of their make-believe house, the large kitchen with the butcher-block island and the scent of herbs, and added a high chair to the blank wall beside the fireplace. Except the kitchen in that house didn't exist. The tense woman bending over the child she'd scooted close to a Formica tabletop in a roadside motel represented both the dream and the reality.

Watching her break the remains of their shared breakfast into small pieces for Allie, Alec realized that he'd drifted for two years on the illusion of a life they could have shared. He'd survived the lonely nights, the long grueling hours of physical therapy, the seemingly endless pursuit of her murderers, on the fiction that if only

Cait hadn't been killed, his life—*their* life—would have been normal.

He'd have worked missions by day and come home to that two-story country house at night. They'd have raised kids and dogs, and eaten fried chicken and high-cholesterol picnics in the summer beneath oaks, maples and spreading chestnut trees, and burned fragrant wood in the fireplace in the winter, holding each other, describing their respective days.

"There's more," Cait said. "You don't have to go so fast."

Though he knew the words weren't meant for him, he felt flayed by them nonetheless. There wasn't more. That was the illusion, this was the reality.

And they had to do something very fast or Cait and Allie might be hurt.

He was the FBI agent. The danger came from his friends. So it wasn't really a case of "they" had to do something—*he* had to. He had to call the press, stage a showdown.

He had to save Cait. And Allie. He had to save his family. Even if they weren't really his.

Cait felt Alec's tension from where she hovered over Allie. He hadn't looked at her from the time Allie poked her finger in his eye and she'd involuntarily laughed, not at his pain, of course, but at the stunned expression on his face. And at his complete lack of knowing what on earth Allie so adamantly demanded he provide.

She didn't say anything to him now, not knowing how to bridge the tremendous gap that stretched between them. They were past the point where wonder over their respective survival was anything but old shocking news. They'd eaten together, slept in the same motel room, stolen a car together. Those things alone, ordinary and bizarre, should have drawn them closer somehow.

Instead, each minute together seemed to solidify the chasm between them. Instead of feeling steadily more at ease, more comfortable in his presence, she felt greater and greater alarm, her limbs governed by awkwardness, her heart pounding in unsyncopated rhythm.

She tried telling herself it was only natural to feel confused by seeing him. She tried reassuring herself that any woman would feel disoriented encountering a man she'd thought dead and buried, but she knew what she felt wasn't just off balance. She felt completely turned inside out.

Too aware of him, she discovered she was afraid of the very chemistry that flared so seemingly effortlessly between them. That electrical, positive-negative charge crackled and snapped with his every move, and her entire body jangled in response.

And yet, that very chemistry seemed destined to fuse them to those three days so long ago, making the present impossible, rough, uncertain. Then, with nothing to lose and everything to gain, the chemistry had seemed a miracle. Now, with everything to lose, it was difficult to understand how attraction could provide anything but trouble.

Their imminent death had provided the fragile foundation between them two years ago. Now, nothing but one sweet and helpless little girl seemed to offer such a bridge.

Still . . . Cait's lips burned with the memory of his kiss and her fingers trembled with the need to trace the planes of his face, the strength of his jaw.

And her mind clamored for stability, for surcease from her restless thoughts.

She felt a wave of gratitude when he clicked on the television set; the noise, the cool, impersonal voice-over for a shampoo commercial pierced her thinking, demanding she listen to exhortation for things outside her unusual life, her uncertain present. He roamed the channels until he found a local all-news network.

Allie ate while the two adults watched the latest-breaking stories in the Washington area. Cait only half listened to both the television and her daughter. The announcer related the latest developments in the New York hostage situation—negotiations were still under way to secure the hostages' release—and Allie loudly described the taste of the orange and apple slices.

"And in a quiet neighborhood in Bethesda, Maryland, neighbors and police are puzzling over the disappearance of a software designer and her infant daughter."

The scene cut to a reporter standing in front of Cait's town house garage. Behind her police officers were interviewing neighbors, measuring the dimensions of the demolished garage door and stringing yellow crime scene tape across her driveway.

"Oh, my God," Cait said, staring at the television. The damage looked far worse in the light of day than it had by night. Her garage door hung at a crazy angle, black skid marks were clearly visible on her otherwise blank driveway.

The reporter said, "Police are still searching for clues to the disappearance of Cait Wilson and her infant daughter. Alerted by neighbors that something was amiss at this quiet address in Bethesda, police responded to the calls at shortly after four o'clock this morning to find both mother and child missing, the garage door torn apart and signs that Wilson and her daughter may have been taken from her house by force."

The camera cut to a prerecorded clip of a police officer describing the condition of Cait's garage. "One of the neighbors who called in a report said she'd seen a man with a gun at Miss Wilson's door about a half an hour before Wilson's car burst through the garage door. A second unknown male was also described as arriving just prior to Wilson's car leaving the area."

"Jack," Alec said.

The reporter came back on the screen. Delia from next door stood with her. Her neighbor gulped back a sob and said, "Cait and I were really close."

Cait groaned.

"She was a really quiet type. And shy. I knew something was up. I mean, she just never had late-night visitors. I should know, I mean, living next door and all. And here were all these people coming to her house in the middle of the night. I told Sean, my husband, to call the police when I saw the first one show up in a taxi. But he said it was none of our business if Cait had midnight callers. I wish I hadn't listened to him. I might have been able to save her. But when the car crashed through the garage...even Sean decided something was wrong. What a terrible noise. Oh, I'm just so worried about her."

Delia gulped again—for air, Cait thought, since Delia had managed that entire speech in less than twelve seconds flat—and held a finger beneath her eye as if crying. "I just hope they're still alive."

Cait suffered a veritable flood of mixed emotions watching her neighbor relating the early-morning escape. "Delia is a twit," she muttered at the same time Alec said, "What a ditz."

Cait felt unable to drag her eyes from the television. She wondered if Aunt Margaret had heard any of this. And irrationally, she worried that people would be tramping through her house, tracking mud on her new carpet, speculating about her emerald nightgown trailing off her bed.

The reporter continued, "Cait Wilson was seen on television only last evening, describing a new software package to be used in the crisis intervention field. Wilson is also a survivor of the terrorist takeover of the World Health Organization two years ago."

The screen faded to black and revealed Cait as she'd appeared on television the night before. Cait glanced over at Alec's still form. His jaw had tightened. "This is what I saw," he said hoarsely. "Last night. When I realized you weren't dead. I thought I was going out of my mind."

She'd felt like that upon seeing him, too. As if she were dreaming, perhaps insane. He'd thought he was going crazy but he'd obviously felt something deeply enough to send him halfway across the country to see her again. She felt a wave of rage at the person or people that were after Alec and now her.

Seen through the motel room television, the camera returned to the on-the-scene reporter then pulled back to show the destroyed garage door again. The police were talking with a clean-cut man of medium height, a bureaucrat sporting the standard gray suit. About fifty, the man with the salt-and-pepper hair held a notebook in one hand and pressed his stomach with the other.

"Cait!" Alec suddenly burst out, pointing at the screen. "That's Jack King. He's at your house right now."

Cait stood up, goose bumps rippling down her spine.

"Police are conferring with FBI experts now, exploring possible connections between the incident two years ago—resulting in the death of a federal agent—and today's disappearance of Ms. Wilson and her infant child. They are asking citizens who may have any information about this case to contact Bethesda authorities or the FBI.''

The reporter turned and walked toward the off-kilter garage door. The camera followed and zeroed in with a moderately long-distance shot of Jack King. Three men stood in the shadow of her garage.

"Jack," Alec said again as a microphone was thrust in his friend's face.

"We're in the preliminary stages of investigating any possible connections between Cait Wilson's disappearance and the incident that took place at the World Health Organization two years ago," Jack King said, facing the camera.

Alec thought the past two years hadn't been terribly kind to Jack King. He carried about forty extra pounds, looked as though he'd slept in his clothes, and frowned as if he were in pain. His white-gray hair accentuated his forty-odd years, making him appear twenty years older than Alec, instead of the five Alec knew to be true.

"Why does the FBI suspect a connection between this disappearance and the incident two years ago?" the reporter asked, though the camera remained on Jack's pained face.

He glanced over his shoulder, as if responding to something said off camera, then looked directly into the lens. "Sources within the bureau are letting us know we now have reason to suspect that the federal agent reportedly killed in the incident is also alive."

"You sorry son of a . . ." Alec muttered.

The reporter holding the microphone seemed similarly affected. The microphone waved, then steadied. "Alive? How could such a mistake have been made?"

Jack King shrugged, though he looked uncomfortable. "Some mistakes are made intentionally," he said without a trace of irony.

"And you believe there's some connection between that agent and Cait Wilson?"

Jack's face seemed to bore into the motel room. Alec felt as if Jack's eyes, staring directly into the camera, were watching him. He felt Cait shiver and put his arm around her waist when she stepped a notch closer to him. He needed to feel her warmth, needed somehow to know she was really there with him.

Jack continued, "An informed source advised the FBI of the possibility that Alec MacLaine is still alive. This same source purports that MacLaine may in fact be responsible, in some part, for the tragic incident at the WHO and, in a more serious implication, might prove to be the engineer behind the White Separatist takeover of that building."

Unconsciously, Cait gripped Alec's shoulder beneath her hand. He'd been in the act of rising, a thundercloud of anger darkening his face. At her touch, he sank back down on the edge of the bed. She scarcely felt his large palm covering her fingers.

"We're double-checking the usual sources," Jack King said with utter seriousness.

Alec sputtered something unintelligible and his hand clenched hers painfully. She could feel the tension coursing through him. It matched her own.

"So, are we to speculate that this former agent—Alec MacLaine?—has kidnapped Wilson and her baby because she survived the incident and might be able to identify him?"

Jack's face as he stared into the camera gave nothing away. "As you say, anything at this point is pure speculation."

Alec's hand over hers gripped so tightly it hurt, but Cait didn't try pulling free.

The reporter stepped into view again. "Police and federal authorities will continue to monitor the situation, searching for any clues leading to the whereabouts of this former hostage victim and her infant daughter." She signed off and the chief announcer came back on to shift to other stories.

Her hand still being squeezed too tightly, Cait remained standing beside Alec, staring at the screen as the announcer took them to another part of the country, another disaster.

Cait couldn't think where to start with her many questions and revelations, stymied by Alec's rigid tension. He sat on the edge of the bed he'd slept in, his body stiff, his face a study in combined fury and shock. He frowned at the set, obviously a million miles away.

Finally Cait shook his hand free and took the remote device from its precarious position on the bed and clicked off the television. She set the remote on the desk and turned to face Alec.

"Start with the day before the hostage incident at the WHO and take me through every single day since."

He looked up at her and smiled that crooked grin of his.

But his eyes were lit with a strange fire, half hopeful, half angry. "Begin at the beginning . . . ?"

"Yes," she said firmly.

She listened carefully as Alec relayed everything he knew, from the start of his investigation into the Aryan Nation separatists through the White Separatist incident at the WHO and his relentless search afterward to discover who had financed and orchestrated it. He spoke without dramatic inflection, but she heard the depth of his feelings nonetheless, perhaps more so because he carefully, studiously kept his voice neutral.

He wrapped up his monologue with, "So, I knew about the cover-up, knew someone in the FBI was responsible for what happened at the WHO two years ago. Then I saw you on television last night—God, was it only last night? It already seems a month ago now—and I rushed to you, bringing danger with me."

Cait nodded. "This is all horrible. But I still don't understand why someone wanted you dead."

Alec shook his head. "I don't have a clue. Until last week, I wouldn't have thought it possible for any one of those three men to be involved at all. I really thought we were working together to ensure those super right-wing operations wouldn't get out of hand."

"If only we had some idea, some glimmer as to why, going to the press with a cover-up story would carry so much more weight," she said, pacing back and forth in front of him.

He reached out and grabbed her, holding on to her cold hands with his own warm, rock-firm fingers. "If we can figure out the motive, maybe we can figure out who the culprit is."

"We know it's not Jack," she said, glancing back at the blank television set. "We just saw him. He's not the man in the suit I saw that day."

"You're right, Cait. It's definitely not Jack," he said, and a strange, rather beautiful smile lit his face. "It's...*not*...Jack."

Cait frowned at him. "But he sure put us in a pickle. You heard him. He just practically accused you of kidnapping me and of setting up the whole thing at the WHO two years ago! He just said the most dreadful things—''

"And the most illuminating."

"What?"

"Cait," he said, standing suddenly, dwarfing her, making her acutely aware of his sheer size, his presence.

He didn't seem to notice though his voice deepened, his tone roughened. "Any partners who work together for years arrange codes. Call it crazy, call it incredibly brilliant. But partner codes sometimes mean the difference between life and death."

"I'm not following you, Alec," she said. But she was in tune with the sharp glint of joy in his eyes, the infusion of adrenaline in his body, the power exuding from him, the feel of his warm hands around hers. For the first time since he'd shown up at her doorstep, she felt a sense of union with him.

"He sent me a definite message during that interview. He used a code we developed years ago. He was trying to warn me."

Apparently unaware of how he was affecting her, he slid his hands up her arms and shook her a little. He paused then, staring at her, and a new wholly exuberant Alec stared at her. "He used the code, Cait. Jack used the damned code."

Alec grinned at her as though the sun had just broken through a tornado-darkened sky. His smile broadened just before he drew her sharply to his chest and kissed her fiercely.

Cait felt her response through every pore of her body. Alec's kiss was no gentle exhortation, no quest to test the turbulent waters between them. This was a hard, demanding statement of vitality, strength and of triumphant awareness.

He let her go almost as swiftly as he'd drawn her close and clapped his hands together before grabbing up the remote control device. "Ha! Jack sent me a signal," he said almost ferociously, waving the remote at her.

Cait stood just inches from him, her body still quivering in reaction to his deep, powerful kiss. She couldn't seem to think.

She smoothed back her hair, stalling for time, stalling for any semblance of rational thought to return. He seemed so happy over that oblique warning, but to Cait there seemed too much he was tossing out without consideration.

She drew a deep breath then forced herself to dampen his enthusiasm. "This Jack, the man you saw, we both saw, in front my garage just now—?"

He interrupted her, still cresting his high. "Damn. I knew it couldn't be him. You don't stand side by side with someone for fifteen odd years and not know them. Fifteen years have to count for something!"

"So it's one of your other friends."

He stopped in midstride, an arrested look on his face, as if she'd just uttered a total non sequitur. "It really threw me when he showed up at your house, though. He must have been trying to bring me in, then. Somehow he knew. Hell, he's known all along. I wonder—"

"Alec—"

"He gave the signal." He looked at her with brightly lit blue eyes. "From the movie *Casablanca*. Corny but effective. 'Round up the usual suspects.' It's the line Louis uses with Humphrey Bogart—Rick—letting Rick escape so he can save Ingrid Bergman and all of France. See? It fits perfectly."

Cait felt a cold chill work down her arms. "Alec, why would he tell that reporter such things?"

"To let me know *he* knows. He's not a threat, don't you see, Cait? We'll have help now," Alec said. He tossed the remote on the bed as if his words cinched the argument.

"So what does the code tell you, Alec?"

"To sit tight and wait. That he's on my side. I know he could still be trying to double-cross me, Cait, but I have this gut feeling that I can trust him."

Cait was never so grateful in her life as to Allie for clamoring for attention at that precise moment. She dampened a washcloth before going to her.

She stepped back onto the strange teeter-totter they shared; the impossible and the mundane. Murder and mothering. She wiped her daughter's face and hands and directed Alec to look around for anything Allie might be able to fit into her mouth.

He looked blankly at her.

"On the floor. Buttons, pins, anything a maid might have missed. She's mainly through the hand-to-mouth stage, but no sense having to rush her to the emergency room at this point. We have enough of an emergency on our hands without having to relearn the intricacies of the Heimlich maneuver on infants."

She felt a rush of sympathy for him as he paled even more and immediately began searching the room for the most minute of potential dangers. He found a spent match in the corner behind an easy chair and held it up in mock triumph. Cait didn't have the heart to break it to him that cardboard and charred sulfur weren't likely to cause any permanent damage to their daughter's health. But after his thorough search, she was satisfied that nothing on the floor could harm Allie. And his searching had given him back a measure of his natural color.

She lifted her daughter from the chair and set her on the ground. She waited until Allie found her legs and tottered toward Alec.

"Man," she said. "Trow."

"At least I'm not Stranger Man anymore," he said, his voice slightly unsteady.

Cait's heart beat erratically as she watched Allie reach her father's impossibly long legs and tug at his trousers. "Up," she demanded.

Cait's heart constricted as Alec glanced from Allie to Cait, as if asking permission. So much, too much, had been stolen from them. He shouldn't have to query her about lifting his daughter into his arms. That should be a right, a gift between him and Allie only. What should she tell her daughter to call Alec? Father? Daddy?

He was her father. By blood, by genetics. But he wasn't her daddy. He'd only seen her for the first time early that morning. Daddy was an endearment born of time, designated out of love, respect and trust.

She waited until he settled Allie in the crook of his arm and obligingly waggled his eyebrows for her, before saying, "All right. Let's suppose that your friend Jack is not the one who's been funding the separatists. Let's suppose it was one of the other two men you know."

Allie slapped at her father's face, trying to get him to move his eyebrows by sheer force.

"We have to suppose that," he said. "And I've got to go get a newspaper right away. If one of us ever gets in trouble and needs help outside the usual channels, we run an ad in the personals."

"How original," Cait said dryly but with a faint smile.

"Well, if something works, you don't change it," he said. "Besides, you can always get a date if you can't get help."

"Is it possible that Jack would go along with a cover-up of such magnitude?"

"Maybe he was like me, maybe he only just found out."

"And maybe he's in on it," she said. She held up a hand to forestall his interruption. "Not innocent, but not evil. Maybe he let us both live because he's basically a nice man. And he doesn't want to see you hurt for the same reason. So he gives you fair warning that he's going to let you go. Even as he crucifies your good name."

Alec stood utterly still, something not to Allie's liking. She continued lightly slapping his brow to get his eyebrows moving while shouting, " 'Gin!' "

Cait had to turn away to hide her smile as Alec did as his daughter asked. Here they were discussing men who hired killers, talking about people who orchestrated terrorism, while indulging a toddler's demand for play.

For Allie, at just over a year, such horrors as murder—and a jagged-edged tension between two adults—didn't have any meaning. She only wanted her father's thick eyebrows to wiggle up and down so she could laugh.

Cait's smile faded at the realization that Allie's innocent game could be ended at any second. There was a very real chance that whichever of Alec's fellow agents wanted him dead would succeed. She instinctively knew that they wouldn't hesitate to use either Allie or herself to get to Alec. And that the only way anyone would get to her would be over Alec's dead body.

And Alec had died for her once already.

"Aunt Margaret," she said.

"What?"

"We have to call Aunt Margaret." She reached for the phone and had the receiver in her hand before he could stop her. But his large hand covered hers and he pressed it back to the set.

"You can't call her," he said quietly.

"I have to. She'll have seen or heard the news about me disappearing. She'll be worried sick."

"Cait . . . whichever one of them is after you, whether it's Jack or one of the others, they'll be waiting for us to call her. We're talking about people from the FBI. My people. If anyone knows how they operate, it's me. They'll already know about her."

"But—"

"Cait, we're not dealing with a couple of small-time hoods. These are trained federal agents."

Cait blanched. "Is she in any danger?"

"I wouldn't think so, no. But we can't risk contacting her. For your sake."

"We have to," she said far more calmly than she felt. "I won't let her worry. And besides, we need her."

"What? Why?"

"To take care of Allie—"

"But we—"

"In case anything happens to you."

Alec fell silent, though he didn't take his hand from hers. Allie leaned out from him, reaching for her mother. Cait took her daughter almost absently, acutely conscious of Alec's warm hand covering hers.

Alec's fingers wrapped around hers. He lifted her hand from the receiver and on to his lips. He turned her hand palm upward and, without taking his eyes from hers, pressed a kiss in the sensitive center. A shiver of reaction flash-fired through her.

"I won't let anything happen to you," he vowed, his hot breath fanning her palm.

Tears stung her eyes. Her knees felt weak. Chemistry, promises, past and present. Too little, too late, and frightening her, far too much, too soon.

"You can't promise that," she said unsteadily.

"I *am* promising just that," he said.

A tear spilled free and snaked down her cheek.

"Mamatry?" Allie asked, patting the tear away.

Cait linked gazes with Alec, feeling the connection to her depths. "I thought you were killed two years ago. You thought I was. What if something like that happens again? What would happen to Allie?"

He let go of her hand, not releasing her gaze. His face was pale and his eyes haunted. Cait could see that every scrap of training in him fought with his instincts; the need to solely protect them warred with the understanding that in the present situation, safeguarding her might not be possible.

He closed his eyes, opened them on Allie. He lightly stroked his daughter's dark curls before shifting his tortured gaze back to Cait.

"I can't call anyone else for help," he said, sounding anguished by the confession. "I don't dare just call Jack, and there's no one I can trust anymore."

Cait drew a deep, ragged breath. He couldn't have spoken words more designed to break her heart.

Chapter 11

Alec knelt beside the makeshift crib, rubbing Allie's back and murmuring a soporific, monotoned litany of go-to-sleep phrases. He'd asked to perform this job, as much to connect with his daughter as to escape the tension with Cait and to avoid her unspoken pleas to once again review their modest plans for escape.

He'd called two of the larger newspapers in the Washington, D.C., metropolitan area and handed them silver-plated tips. He'd done the same with all three major network affiliates in the region.

It had daunted him to think his gift of the tips wasn't taken with wild enthusiasm. The reporters he'd talked to weren't like reporters in the movies; they wanted the entire story handed to them, fed line by line, word by word. And even with all he'd told them, the separatist angle, the dead-not-dead twist, they had seemed blasé about the story.

He should have realized in this era following Watergate, the Iran-Contra affair and a host of others, a coverup was old hat, common fare for reporters whose palates required greater and greater amounts of seasoning. He shouldn't have tried offering appetizers, he should have leapt in with the highly spiced main dish: two years ago someone in the FBI murdered the terrorists and, secondhand, the hostages, after setting up the entire scenario to begin with. That might have grabbed them. Or it might have made them hang up on what they would assume was a nut case. Short of revealing his identity and offering them proof in the form of documentation—not to mention Cait and Allie—he was left with their painful apathy. Because he couldn't offer the proof without handing Cait over to whoever wanted to kill her.

God, what a mess. For ten cents he'd pack Cait and the baby into the stolen sedan and drive into the sunset, getting as far away from all this as possible. Not New Mexico—his pals would look for them there—but somewhere. They could change their names, pull together some form of a life. If living in constant fear of discovery—and murder—could be called a life.

And if that wasn't a pipe dream, what was? He didn't even know how Cait felt about him anymore. Perhaps he'd never known. She'd never said, then, and she didn't seem inclined to voice her feelings now. Hell, he wasn't even sure how he felt. There was too much of the past separating them, days when they should have been getting to know one another, learning the little things that comprised a relationship, developing inside jokes and outside commonalities.

Every time he looked at her, he felt an ache deep inside his chest, as though her slender, lovely form radiated some jagged electricity that sent sparks of pain through him. He wanted to rail against the sheer unfairness of their separation, and worse, their reunion.

And now they would be complicating things even more, because hours after Cait had brought it up he'd reluctantly given in to her demands to contact her aunt Margaret.

He was adamant on the point that the FBI would very likely have a tail on Aunt Margaret and would know something was up should she try going anywhere outside her daily routine.

"So we go there," Cait had countered.

That was the last place they needed to go. His friends would expect her to do just that. The bushes at her aunt Margaret's place were probably crawling with field agents.

But Cait had finally convinced him that she knew her aunt's habits so well, it needn't appear Aunt Margaret was doing anything out of the ordinary. They could easily connect with Aunt Margaret and pass her Allie without anyone being the wiser.

"She volunteers at the animal shelter on Mondays and Fridays. We'll be waiting for her."

Alec had scoffed, but Cait had blithely ignored his arguments. "It'll work, Alec. She'll recognize my voice. She's always taking animals home. She'll come. She can take Allie home in a dog carrier. No one will be the wiser."

Alec felt torn apart at the notion of separating Allie from Cait and vice versa. And he could see the struggle Cait was making with the hard decision, as well. But he had to admit she was right; if something did go wrong,

Allie had to be safe. And no matter what happened to
him or Cait, there would be no reason for his friends to
go after Aunt Margaret and Allie.

But, worried that her aunt Margaret would suffer far
too much anxiety if she wasn't assured her niece and
great-niece were safe, Alec played with Allie while Cait
pretended to be a friend of her aunt's calling to ask Margaret if she'd had any word from Cait. As she'd known
would happen, her aunt recognized her immediately. And
before she'd hung up, Cait had managed to convey a hint
of their plan.

At his questioning look, Cait had smiled tremulously
and informed him that aunts and nieces had codes and
signals also.

She'd held Allie tightly against her after the phone call
and Alec had the wrenching feeling she was already saying goodbye. He hadn't been around his daughter more
than a few hours, but already he knew how painful a
separation from her would be. How much stronger that
fear and pain must be for Cait.

Somehow, arranging Allie's safety struck Alec—and
probably Cait as well, to judge by the bleak expression on
her face—as an admission of failure, as if tucking Allie
away was to admit he couldn't protect them.

But they wouldn't be handing the baby over to Aunt
Margaret until Monday. That gave them roughly a day
and a half to do nothing but wait and spend time together. Alec couldn't help but think of the similarity to
the past. They'd had only days together then. Only days
now.

Each second that passed seemed monumentally swift,
profound in an intensity of emotion, but going too fast.
Once Cait had finally let Allie go, he'd held her tightly
himself, needing the contact with his daughter, needing

to forge some bond that would see him through the time of separation from her.

He felt like the yo-yo Allie used for a greeting, pulled two ways simultaneously. Danger, child's play... fear, wonder.

Allie's eyes grew heavier and heavier though she obviously wanted to fight her body's demand for a nap. Cait had told him that she would just go down and fall right asleep if she took her into the alcove and placed her in bed. But after the time spent playing with her, eating lunch with her, even reading her a delightfully silly rhyming book, *What Do You Give a Butler for His Birthday?*, he wanted to share the moment his little girl turned baby again and drifted into dreams.

Her left forefinger crooked and slipped into her mouth and Alec's chest tightened. He remembered his mother describing his doing exactly the same thing as a child. Were such mannerisms genetic? Inherited memory? Were children who sucked fingers different than those who sucked thumbs? What would she become as she grew older, what would her personality be as a teenager, a young woman, a mother of her own?

Without conscious awareness, his words shifted from meaningless soothers to heartfelt promises. "And when you go to school, if anybody ever bothers you, you just let me know and I'll stop that nonsense. And if you ever need to just talk, if you're worried about something, or if you're feeling lonely, I'll be as close as you want me to be."

His hand, tanned from his months in the New Mexico mountains, scarred with half a dozen nicks and scrapes, looked enormous on her fragile back. He had spent the morning and most of the afternoon holding her, fascinated with her, playing with her, and knew she wasn't as

fragile as he'd assumed at first. But seeing his hand on
her now, spanning the full length of her torso, the contrast between them was all the more noticeable.

He was so deeply and irrevocably in love with his
daughter that he knew he would never be the same man
he used to be. This fathomless, intense emotion marked
him, branded him, tied him to her forever and longer.

Cait fought the tears that stung her eyes. Less than six
feet from the alcove, she heard every word, each promise Alec uttered to his sleepy—and by this time, sleeping—daughter.

In a more perfect world, all his promises would come
true. And in that lovely perfect place, she herself would
melt into his embrace and all other details would fall into
sweet order. They would, as they had in her loss-driven
fantasies, slide into a blissful parenthood, lovers and
caretakers, husband and wife, drifting aimlessly and
lovingly through the dream-filled days.

No one would be waiting somewhere to kill Alec, he
would forget he had ever carried a gun, all bad guys
would forever disappear from the face of the earth.

"Cait?"

She looked up at the man who did carry a gun, even if
he stashed it on top of the television cabinet to keep it out
of Allie's precocious reach.

She'd shared every single second of the time with him
since she woke in her town house certain something was
wrong. She'd watched him steal a car, play with Allie, eat
breakfast and lunch, she'd even seen him peel his clothing free and she'd lain only a few feet from him, listening to the steady rumble of his chest as he slept. But now
she wondered if she had ever truly seen Alec the man be-

fore, either in the two-year-old past or in the short twelve
hours she'd shared with him.

Her fantasies suddenly seemed flat and lifeless. Pretty,
yes, but so removed from any semblance of reality that
they lacked depth or sustaining interest. For the first time
she wondered if it mightn't be so bad that they were
strangers. Strangers met, learned to know each other, and
sometimes, however rarely, two strangers fell in love.

She didn't know what showed on her face, what thread
of her scattered emotions spilled free and lured him to her
side. But he walked slowly toward her, one steady step at
a time.

She pushed to her feet, her hands pressed against her
sides, her heart thundering in her suddenly constricted
chest.

Whatever thoughts tumbled in his head, his eyes blazed
with hunger, his unsmiling lips parted with direct inten-
tion. She knew he would kiss her, knew she wanted him
to, no matter how much it scared her to repeat the past.
They'd been in danger then and had succumbed to passion. They were in danger now.

But there were differences. Subtle, perhaps, refining
and gentled, but differences nonetheless.

She didn't try to sidestep, couldn't be coy or pretend
shyness with him. Too much had happened between them
two years before, and too much lay between them now to
hide behind pretense.

He lowered his lips to hers. And if the kiss tasted of
uncertainty, it was still roughly honest. She didn't know
what revelations had struck him as he lulled Allie to sleep,
but instinctively understood that he had as great a need
as she to solidify something between them, a need perhaps to make the present concrete.

He drew her into his arms, gently, and part of her remembered how very well they fit together, the hard planes of his body against her softer curves, her head just at the apex of his shoulder, his mouth reachable if she so much as lifted her lips, leaving her throat vulnerable to his touch, his caress.

He lowered his lips to the throbbing pulse at her collarbone and lightly traced the thready rhythm in the vein with the tip of his tongue. She shuddered but didn't, couldn't, tear herself away from him. Her fingers splayed, her body instinctively arched toward him and he caught and held her close.

"Ah, Cait..." he said with a ragged note of longing in his deep voice. "I don't know how to turn back the clock. I wish I could."

"What's happened is past, Alec," she told him, and raised her trembling fingers to his face. "It's neither good nor bad, it's just past."

He nodded, staring down at her, his blue eyes dark with unspoken emotion. "The two years without knowing her tear me apart," he said. "Do you hate me for not being there?"

"No," she said. "I could never hate you, Alec."

"We'll get through this somehow."

He used the plural as if it were natural to assume a togetherness. There wasn't any together to assume.

"Those years are gone and nothing we can ever do will call them back," she said, more for her own benefit than his.

"But I still want you, Cait. That much survived." His hands tightened at her waist, drawing her even closer.

His raw honesty stripped any semblance of coherency from her. She raised her lips instead, a question and answer both.

He kissed her almost roughly, demandingly, as seemingly desperate as she to put paid to the past, to establish this moment as the present only. To forge a new bond between them.

She responded to his kiss with every fiber of her being. She shivered as if cold, trembled as if afraid, but in truth she was overwarm and strangely calm. It was as if she were coming home, not to that fantasy dream house in the country, but to where she'd always belonged, in his arms, feeling his ragged breathing, hearing his heart thundering in his breast, inhaling his sweet-sharp male scent.

She didn't know what she felt about him—her emotions were too confused, too conflicting. But in his arms, with his lips pressed against hers, she didn't have to think, didn't have to analyze, didn't have to understand. Drowning in his kiss, in his scent and taste, the feel of his hands on her body, the velvet-soft pressure of his lips and tongue, she could just drift, allow the moment to engulf her, the past to fade and the present to solidify.

With a groan he raised her from the floor and lowered her to the bed tucked in the corner of the bedroom, the bed she'd curled up on, falling asleep to the lulling rhythm of his breathing.

She half felt she should say something, anything, but his lips seized hers again and all words fled as she drowned in his kiss, in the feel of his firm body pressed to hers. Slowly, as if reluctant to leave the taste of her lips, he kissed her chin, the sensitive hollow at the base of her throat, coming back to her trembling lips, and dropping back to kiss her shoulders through her blouse, blowing hot, moist air against her responsive skin.

She arched against him, closing her eyes.

"Ah, Cait..." he breathed against the valley between her suddenly aching breasts. As if aware she was drifting from the present, slipping into that nowhere land 'twixt now and then, he stopped his progress and raised his head. She opened her eyes to meet the cautious hunger in his.

To touch him now was to let him know the extent of her want. To reach out for him was tantamount to accepting him in this strange present, accepting the loss of the two years that lay so unalterably between them, and to admitting that what they had found two years ago wasn't irretrievably buried.

Not to touch him would be to condemn her to forever wondering.

Slowly, her hands shaking so badly that she felt their vibrations to the deepest recesses of her heart, she raised her fingers to his face, not closing her eyes, but watching his squeeze shut as if her fingers burned him. The muscles in the hollows of his cheeks drew taut and flexed beneath her light touch.

"Oh, Alec..." she murmured.

Without opening his eyes, he smiled as if at a tender memory and his face shifted under her fingers.

The smile, the feel of it against her hands, the acceptance inherent in it, tipped her over some precipice of rationality. Everything in the two years of loneliness told her she shouldn't lower her hands to tug at his sweatshirt, to plunge her hands into the intense heat that hovered between his shirt and his silken skin. But nothing in the world could have stopped her.

He lay still, stretched out beside her, deadly serious now, his eyes raking her face, asking too many questions, revealing far too much for her to consider.

Alec felt his heart become a completely separate entity within him, one struggling furiously for freedom; it hammered against his chest with wild abandon. His hands, normally as steady as the proverbial rock, trembled like a kid's upon a first kiss.

Cait's eyes had darkened to emerald with her want. Her lips were full and moist, an invitation and a command he obeyed without question. He felt certain he could die right then and there and never regret a moment of his life. And he was equally certain that everything in his life had been meant for this single moment.

Whatever they'd found and lost in that dismal closet two years ago no longer seemed to matter. It was now that held meaning, the silken feel of Cait's hands on his bare arms, the sweet taste of her dewy lips, the passion imperfectly banked in her quivering body: this was meaning, this superseded anything in the past.

Her eyelids flickered down, as if she were in pain, but her fingers clung to him, holding him over her. Her body arched upward, meeting his, rousing him to sheer insanity by her artless need. He muttered a curse and thrust his arm behind her to hold her against him, to keep her there.

She murmured something but her words were inchoate. Alec hesitated, waiting for explanation, but she wrapped her fingers around his shoulders and drew him closer still. He was grateful for the dim daylight in the room. He needed to see her, to be with her in the now, in the present. Their times before had always occurred in the pitch darkness.

He needed to see her face, to see her beautiful body, to watch her reaction to his kisses, his touch. They had never dared touch each other in the light two years before. Then, the dark had served as a pseudo security blanket; as long as they couldn't see each other, no one else would be able to, either.

Here in the light, with the doors locked from the inside this time, the baby asleep, no one aware of where they were, he could make her cry with his tenderness, make her cry out with his caresses. And she could see how very much he ached for her, how strongly she affected him, how she made him feel alive.

Alec released his fierce hold of her, letting her slip back down against the soft mattress. She stared up at him in heavy-lidded bemusement and yet a gentle smile curved her full lips.

It was well and fine to need the present and the present only, but the past couldn't be ignored, couldn't be switched off like the light he craved now. "Cait, I'm so sorry—"

Her fingers sealed the words within his lips and he realized she'd guessed something of what he might say.

"When we were together two years ago," she murmured, "we found a passion that could take away the fear. It was like a drug—"

"A marvelous narcotic."

"Yes, just like that. We knew we were going to die, and that passion took away the pain of that knowing."

Alec was almost afraid to ask. Afraid to hope. "And now?"

"And now we're together."

He knew he should explore that cryptic comment, the many things it *didn't* say, but she snaked her hand to the nape of his neck and drew him down to her lips for another taste, another kiss. And her fingers inched beneath his hair, making goose bumps rise on his back, more effectively forcing him to the present than any lengthy discussion could ever have done. He found he could ignore the might-have-beens, the should-have-been-saids.

Cait didn't want logic or explanations. Instinctively she understood this was a very precarious present, that what linked them together now was as uncertain as a stormy night in the desert; it might rain torrents with lightning and huge claps of thunder, or it could be blown away on a freezing wind. She'd lost too much already. She deserved . . . *they* deserved . . . this oh-so-precious moment. Together.

When Allie woke, needing dinner and tending, when Aunt Margaret would be met, when plans needed to be made, when futures forced their unwelcome presence between them, that would be time enough to study the past, time for regrets, revelations and possible recriminations, but now she only wanted his body pressing against hers, his hands rousing her to mindlessness.

As if in tune with her thinking, which he'd always, *always* been able to do, Alec rolled her over and positioned her astride his long body. He lifted shaking hands to her blouse and slowly began unbuttoning the garment. One by one, he freed each button, not opening her blouse yet, but drawing out the moment when she would feel, could watch him gazing at her. Alec tugged her blouse from her trousers and continued his slow, deliberate unfastening. When finished, including the two at her wrists, he smiled, as if satisfied with his task.

His eyes rose to hers. He kept them there as he pushed her blouse from her shoulders, letting it slide down her arms and pool at her hands. And kept them linked with hers as he lowered his fingers to unhook her bra. And maintained that gaze as he slowly drew the blouse and silky straps free and tossed the last remaining barrier aside.

Only then did Alec lower his eyes and, as he had earlier that day when he had only kissed her and nothing more, he made no move to raise his hands to touch her. She understood, though it made her shiver; he wanted to study her, to memorize her, to know her as intimately by sight as he'd known her in the dark before.

Beneath his regard, her nipples grew hard and her breasts seemed to swell and ache for his touch. She shivered again, not from any sense of cold, but rather from the opposite, as if she were on fire. Alec raised his hands then and gently laid them on her shoulders, gripped them fiercely for a moment, then released her to trail his fingers down the full length of her arms and back up again. And over, grazing her collarbone, and lower, to follow the full line of her breasts. He cupped both gently, raising them, then palming them, rubbing her hardened nipples against his lightly callused hands.

She shuddered and closed her eyes as he raised her up, shifting her forward. And bit back a moan as he took one nipple between his lips and laved it with a hot, knowing tongue. His hands, gentle and tender, kneaded her back, exhorting her to rock into him. Then, as she fell into a rhythm as primal as nature itself, his hands firmed in their exploration, stroking her back with long, sure caresses. His suckling intensified, switching back and forth from breast to breast in avid attention.

With a groan of pure need, Alec rolled her over, straddling her now, his eyes taking in every inch of her bared skin.

"You are so incredibly beautiful," he said. He made her believe it was true, and she felt the power such words could give infuse her veins with languor, making her legs lax with the need to feel him against her.

Two years ago she'd been half terrified of her tremendous response to him, had attributed it over the lonely months of his absence to a syndrome prisoners often succumbed to, that of feeling deep emotional or physical bonds with fellow inmates. She'd had only two choices, the pretty dream or the sick syndrome. But she wasn't dreaming now, nor was she a prisoner. The lights were on and they had control of their environment. And that same scalding passion caught her and shook her, holding her in its fierce and demanding thrall.

Alec, as snared by Cait's sensuality as by her passion, caught in the wonder of the myriad emotions he saw flicker across her features, found he could no longer be content with seeing only half of her; he had to see everything. To know everything about her.

He forced himself to go slowly, and held his breath to steady the hands unfastening her trousers. She quivered at his touch and he rasped out her name. He'd remembered her touch, her responsive questing hands, but he'd forgotten what it felt like to drown in her. The circumstances were different, altered enough so that even the gift of her body seemed freer, changed.

Danger lurked outside the doors like prowling wolves just waiting for a chance to catch them unaware. And somehow, feeling Cait's fingers unbuckling his belt, the danger wasn't outside, it was here, now, a possible future unfolding as surely as his pants unzipped.

They could turn back. Stop this sweet madness. And slowly, carefully try to build a future from a rocky, uncertain present. That would be the wise thing to do. That would be prudent, responsible. Smart.

Her hand slid beneath the band of his shorts and sheathed him. He groaned aloud and shifted off her to tug at her trousers, sending a silent prayer of thanks to the manufacturers of loose-fitting pants. He tossed them to the other bed and moments later his own pants joined them, legs intertwined every bit as much as their human counterparts.

There were so many things he would like to do for her, tasting her, thrusting her over the edge of endurance long before his own rush to that precipice. But Cait's legs parted and she begged him, her voice husky and raw, to come inside her, to join her, to take her over that cliff while holding her close.

Alec could no more have resisted that plea than push her off a real ledge. He raised himself above her, poised, gazing into her eyes, needing her, wanting her, afraid of losing the past, terrified of the future, but aching for her now.

"Please," she murmured, and reached her hands to his hips, drawing him forward, guiding him.

There was something he had to do, something he needed to think about. But he couldn't think with Cait arching up to meet him, capturing him, drawing him into her.

He groaned aloud and shuddered with exquisite pain-like ecstasy. And remembered what it was he needed to do. He pulled free, up and out of her, reality washing him like icy water.

"What—?" Cait called out, reaching for him.

"Allie," he said.

"She's asleep."

He turned and lowered his forehead to his hands, thinking. "No. I know that. But last time...we didn't...and you had Allie."

"Oh, I see," Cait murmured, but Alec could have sworn he heard a note of amusement in her voice. He felt her wriggle across the bed and fish in Allie's diaper bag.

She held out a wrapped condom and waited until he reached for it to drop it into his nerveless fingers.

He looked at her, not even beginning to know what he felt.

"I was a Girl Scout," she said.

A smile tugged at his lips. "I thought it was Boy Scouts who were supposed to be prepared. My hands are shaking too much to open the damned thing," Alec said.

"And mine aren't?" she asked.

"How about if I open it and you put it on?"

"Do you trust me?" she asked.

And with her question, any awkwardness was past them. "Yes," he said, and though he couldn't have begun to let her know how much he truly trusted her, what all that implied in his life, he lifted the plastic covering to his teeth and gave a little tug to rip it open.

She wasn't smiling as she took the condom from his fingers and lowered her hands to carefully, slowly roll it on. He groaned as she turned the prosaic necessity into a sensual experience.

With a low growl, he grabbed her and shifted her deeper onto the bed. He lowered his lips to hers, recapturing the moment, seizing the present with all the new-found trust and gratitude he could show. He wanted her so badly he ached, but he needed her to match him in that want, to crave his touch, to dig her fingers into his shoulders, drawing him closer, ever closer.

Cait thought Alec's eyes were nearly glassy with longing, flawless in their unalloyed delight in her. As near to drowning as she'd been, his longing sank her even deeper, leaving her gasping for breath.

"Alec..." she whispered into his ear, arching to him, reveling in the naked feel of his flesh against her bare skin. In this rare and poignant present, she felt the scars of his wounds and no longer found them painful to think about; they were only another facet of him.

This was the moment, this was their time. The night could bring some new disaster, the morrow a terrible twist and the future an unknown blank, but now, his hands roaming her body with the sure touch of a sculptor, his kisses sending her places she'd only dreamed of traveling, she seized that time with nearly frantic need.

Alec cupped her breasts and flicked her hardened nipples with his teeth. He traced the curves of her body with his hands and followed the trail with his moist, hot tongue. He drove her crazy, effortlessly, endlessly, making her body shake and her fingers splay on the bed and her legs tremble with longing to wrap around his.

"Oh, please..." Cait begged him again, raising her hands to dig her fingers into his shoulders, drawing him up, pulling him closer.

Through lowered eyes she met his equally entranced gaze. Like her, he was lost in a world of passion, a universe of feeling, of sensation, touch, smell.

He slipped into her and she all but growled, arching to meet him fully. He plunged deep within her and stilled, holding her tightly against him, his eyes locked with hers, his body throbbing, thrumming.

Alec didn't speak and she was grateful for the absence of words. At this moment, during this perfect endless moment, she felt no need for words. They were communicating on some profound, primal level, a place of absolute integration. For however brief and vague a time, they were literally, wordlessly and figuratively one.

He ground his lips to hers as he began to slowly move within her. Pulled back, then in. She lifted her hips to meet him, finding a rhythm that was as natural as heat in the summer and snow in the winter. Rocking with him, captured in his arms, locked with him, she lost all thought, kept in this world by his touch alone.

Cait thought she would like the moment to last forever—the feel of his naked body against hers, the feel of his ragged breathing against the curve of her neck, the slow, rocking rhythm, atavistic in its command. But her own breathing grew more and more shallow, and her body began to thrum as forces gathered to propel her over that precipice only he could take her to.

Her hands held on to him as if she would lose him, and he clung to her with matched ferocity. He began rocking faster, driving deeper, thrusting against her. His hands grasped her shoulders from behind, and his hips ground against her. He was liquid fire and solid steel. Swift, hard, a steady, dizzying meeting.

She felt herself slipping over that edge and clung to him, unwilling to go yet, but unable to stop herself. He cried out suddenly, driving deep within her, calling her name, and freezing, hot, molten against her. He stopped all movement, his body utterly rigid, not even breathing. And plunged her over that precipice, sending her reeling into a universe of shattering splendor.

And was there to catch her and slowly, achingly tenderly gather her back into his arms.

She would worry about the future later, she told herself firmly. Aunt Margaret would join them, Allie would need feeding and changing. The world, with all its duties and dangers, could come crashing in then. But for now, she would rest on Alec's shoulder, her naked body pressed against his, feeling his breathing, listening to his steady heartbeat.

In his arms, her legs tangled in his, she could forget the chasm between them, ignore the past and disregard the future. All trouble would come soon enough. She no longer needed dreams or fantasies about Alec; this single moment with him was fantasy enough.

"Alec?"

"Hmm?"

"What's your middle name?" she asked.

He chuckled slightly, then his breath caught and his arms tightened around her, holding her fiercely to his side. "How did you guess?" he murmured.

"Guess what?"

"That of all the things I regretted about that morning, not telling you my middle name was the one I regretted the most."

"Well?"

"Francis," he said. "Alec Francis MacLaine."

Cait smiled and pressed a kiss to his chest. "No wonder you didn't tell me," she said. "That's perfectly dreadful."

And he laughed out loud, his body thrumming against hers. He rolled over her, pinning her against the bed. "Dreadful?"

"Perfectly," she said.

"And this?" he asked, running his hands down the curve of her waist and lower still.

"Perfect."

Chapter 12

Monday, November 12, 9:45 a.m. EST

For Alec, forty-one hours had passed in a halcyon haze, a sweet blur made all the more poignant by its imminent ending. Every moment spent holding his newfound daughter was etched with diamond clarity on his heart, implanted in his memory. Each glance at Cait's smiling face, every meeting of her green eyes with his lent a rare vibrancy of color to the gray that had become his world.

Locked in the safety of their motel room in Sterling, Virginia, he could afford the luxury of ignoring the future and reveling in the absolute present. Patty-cake and horsey rides took precedence over danger and nebulous futures. Busy-busy bee and itsy-bitsy spider brought laughter and wrenching heartache both and he played the games over and over and over again until his daughter's laughter outweighed the fear of losing her tomorrow.

While Alec bounced Allie on his knees or learned that holding her high above his head wasn't going to result in permanent brain damage for his daughter or heart failure for himself, Cait pored over his copious amounts of data inside his laptop computer, catching up on all the information he knew, searching for a motive, a single connection that would give them any clue as to *why* everything had happened.

In unspoken and unacknowledged agreement, he and Cait hadn't talked about the FBI, separatists, terrorism, or next week. He had only to look for those topics in the shadows beneath her lovely eyes or hear it in the rapid clicking of the computer's keyboard and the silence with which she stared at the data on the screen. And she could see the effects of all of it in his tension every time room service knocked on their door or whenever a fellow guest's silhouette crossed their window.

And they didn't talk about the past, those three days they'd shared staving off fear and death. They didn't share reminiscences about their passion, their tension, or their broken dreams.

They talked about movies they'd seen and liked, books they'd read and loved or hated, places one or the other had seen, visited, or had once upon a time wanted to visit in the pipe-dream days of their youth. He discovered her favorite color was burnt sienna, which struck him as rich in contrast as her pixie face and siren voice. She learned his preference for abstract reality over the purely abstract in the paintings they discussed at length.

And during the night, with Allie in her little bed, the lights low but not completely doused, they pretended they had forever and memorized each detail of the other's body lovingly, tenderly and in absolute harmony.

And if their laughter sometimes seemed forced or their smiles slipped and an unwary slack fear would steal across their features, neither commented on the lapse, for these were stolen moments, time without an anchor. And if neither slept very much, too aware that Monday marked an end to their strange and beautiful present, they at least held each other close, curving into each other like silver spoons in a precious case.

It seemed to Alec that the cruel fate that had brought both of them such pain in the past had taken a kinder turn and was, for the moment, content to allow them peace and privacy. No policeman found the stolen car in the parking lot. The tips he'd given the press weren't headlines or top stories on the local news channels. Even the message he anticipated from Jack King hadn't made its way into the personals yet.

Alec didn't wonder what he'd done to deserve such a miracle of the time; he knew. He'd spent the past two years teetering on the very brink of hell. He'd lived with bitterness and pain so long they had become companions. To set that dreadful pair aside for Cait and Allie seemed a gift beyond price, and he would have given all promise of heaven to extend their time of peace one more day, one more hour.

But all too soon tomorrow morning was Monday and they were taking Allie to Cait's aunt Margaret for safekeeping. With only hours to go before he handed his daughter to what was for him a complete stranger, he had to break their unvoiced ban on discussion of plans, details and the future.

"Cait..." he murmured, drawing her more tightly within his arms. Her warm back nestled against his chest and he had to will his body to be still. "Are you absolutely sure about leaving Allie with your aunt?"

She didn't answer for a long time and he racked his brain for thoughts she might be considering.

"How can I be sure about anything, Alec?" she asked softly and, he thought, sadly. "All I know is that I don't want her with me if someone's trying to kill me. I don't want her hurt."

She didn't have to add "or worse." That terrible thought was all too evident in her tone. He held her close and pressed a kiss to her temple. "I'm so sorry about all this, Cait," he murmured, and at her sigh, wasn't sure if he was apologizing about the danger that awaited them or the few halcyon days they had snatched together.

"If we get out of this, Cait—"

She pulled out of his arms, breaking his vow short. She rolled onto her side to face him. A tear slowly marred the perfect line of her cheek. "Don't talk about the future, Alec," she said. "Please don't make any promises." She raised a trembling hand to his cheek as if to take any sting away from her words.

She couldn't have known how deeply her words cut him. Sometimes a promise was all a man had to give.

"I love you, Cait," he said quietly, and though he hadn't intended to say it, hadn't even thought about the reality of it, he knew, to the very depths of his being, that it was true. He did love her. The way she smiled when she played with Allie, as if the entire universe hung on her daughter's giggle, the way she bravely faced the dangers surrounding her, her temper, her laughter, her honesty, her little turned-up nose and the way she called his name in the height of passion.

She didn't say anything. She only closed her eyes as if his admission had brought her pain, not pleasure.

"I want us to have a future together, Cait. A real future. A home, a life—"

"Stop!" she cried out, sounding agonized beyond torture.

She shut him out by covering her face with her slender hands.

He swiftly hitched himself up to his elbow and bent over her, prying her fingers free. "Cait?"

"Stop, Alec, just stop!"

"What is it?"

She opened tear-drenched eyes to gaze up at him. The extent of her pain, and knowing he'd caused it, felt like a knife blade between his ribs.

"Cait..."

She said raggedly, "You can't talk about a future together. We don't even have a past, damn it. You tell me you love me, but you don't even *know* me. I don't know you! You just met your daughter for the first time two days ago. Days, Alec. That's all we had then, that's all we've had now! I can't talk about a future when all the time we've shared amounts to a handful of snatched minutes."

"Ah, Cait—"

"Minutes, Alec. Minutes waiting for doors to open and bad guys to come crashing through. Minutes knowing that every one of them might be our last. You might be used to that, trained for it, even enjoy it. But I can't live like this. I hate it. I hate it, do you understand? Today I'm handing Allie over to Aunt Margaret because I'm afraid, I'm *terrified*, I won't be able to keep her safe as long as she's with you and me! And you tell me you love me. God, Alec, love can't matter now. Just surviving is all I can think about now. Just hoping there will be a tomorrow for me to be able to hold Allie again. Just hoping I'm around for her."

She gave a great sob and tried pushing him away. He felt like crying, too, burying his head in the hollow of her neck and just letting go. But he quelled her struggles by dragging her into his arms and holding her firmly, tightly, wishing he could hold on to her forever, keep her warm and safe.

Cait knew she was being unfair. But nothing about the situation between them was fair. They'd passed the time waiting for Monday in a rare and strangely beautiful denial. Alec's wanting to talk about a future—something neither of them could afford to bank on—brought the curtain down on the act.

Her heart was breaking. In a matter of hours she would be handing her daughter over to her aunt, and no matter how loving Aunt Margaret would be, Cait would remember the pain of the necessity of leaving Allie behind every day for the rest of her life.

But it wasn't only Allie she cried for. She cried because Alec had told her he loved her. A thousand, million times she'd imagined him saying exactly those words, had heard herself answering in kind.

She didn't doubt he believed them. She believed them. But words of love only served to underscore the tenuousness of their time together. He wanted a future, but they didn't have one. Even if, by some miracle, they survived the efforts of a seemingly crazed FBI agent, how could she think about a future with a man whose entire way of life constituted danger, fear, bullets and guns?

She could see in these past two days that Alec had seemingly forgotten how dangerous he looked with his shoulder holster on, how hard he could appear when someone knocked at the door or simply got out of a car. Seeing him on the floor, flat on his back, his daughter bouncing on his chest, the two of them atonally chanting a line from a television commercial, it was difficult to remember the other Alec MacLaine—the agent in charge, the highly trained professional. With Allie he seemed much like any other good father—tender, kind, endlessly patient, affectionate and warm.

Allie had called him Stranger Man. He was that and more, he was an agent. Agent Man. Agent Daddy.

Cait didn't have to tell him that guns and diapers wouldn't mix. She'd seen his acceptance of her need to get Allie to a safe place while the dangers still surrounded them. And she'd seen the pain in him at the need to admit he couldn't guarantee his daughter's safety.

But he held her now, so tightly it almost hurt, murmuring her name, pressing his generous lips to her temple, her forehead, soothing her as if she were a child devastated by some disaster that tore a little bit of the innocence away.

"It'll be all right, Cait. I promise, it'll be all right."

But Cait knew he was lying.

The drive through the beautiful Virginia countryside was quiet and uneventful, a couple taking in the scenery with their daughter, except that a tension rode along with them, breeding greater and greater amounts of anxiety with every passing mile.

For all that Cait didn't believe that Alec really could promise things being all right, she nonetheless repeated his vow like a litany against the uncertain future. She clung to the words with every fiber of her being. And, unconsciously, clung to Alec.

The miles to Kitty Hawk, North Carolina, seemed to whip by, and all too soon she could smell the salty tang of the ocean, could see the gray-blue grasses that presaged the silken-soft beaches. Though the sands were empty during the off-season, the gulls still patrolled the highways, swooping down at the car as if asking what delectable treats these autumn comers might have in store for them.

Nag's Head, a city with a small-town atmosphere, charmed tourists by the thousands each spring and summer and still managed to appear quaint in the cold, stormy-gray days of autumn and winter. Beach cottages, boarded up for the off-season, looked forlorn and wistful, and tall, elegant condominiums along the waterfront seemed abandoned, like relics from another, more gracious era.

Alec echoed her thoughts, a knack that still had the ability to rock her. "It's beautiful even in gray," he said. A half smile played on his lips, but he didn't appear anything but sad.

Something stirred in her that she couldn't identify. A quickening, a low hum of discomfort that rippled across her shoulders and tingled deep within her. Did she love him? Was that what the strange sensation was? No, this was an ache, a pain of some kind, made worse by its lack of identification.

Before crossing the Virginia border they had once again stolen a car. Alec had pulled the sedan in to a parking space at a large shopping mall and had found another car with keys in it within a matter of minutes. Thirty miles later he'd stolen yet another set of plates and switched them with the tags on their new acquisition, a compact Chevrolet.

They'd also stopped at a department store and picked out wigs, a few items of clothing, some extras for Allie, a medium-sized pet carrier and a remarkably realistic toy dog that wriggled all over when a button was pressed on his belly. Allie loved it.

Alec drove the car around the block several times before deciding the area looked devoid of FBI. But to be on the safe side, he turned the car over to Cait some three blocks from the animal shelter. He helped her arrange a sleeping Allie in a makeshift bed inside the pet carrier, then, with a long, lingering look at Cait, sauntered down the street in a loose-gaited, easy stride, his long, blond hair blowing softly in the breeze and a wriggling Lhasa apso in his arms.

Cait shook her hands several times to get them to stop shaking, then finally put the car in gear. It was hard not to slow the Chevrolet when she passed Alec and harder still not to stare at him in the rearview mirror. Even she, who had spent every moment with him during the past two and a half days, wouldn't have recognized him.

She hoped she was equally disguised. Her wig was a honeyed gold in color and brushed against her neck. And she wore a pair of simple, wire-framed glasses that did nothing more to her vision than obscure it with the unfamiliarity of wearing them.

She pulled to the front of the animal shelter as if she came there on a regular basis. After retrieving the pet carrier and her still-sleeping daughter from the back seat, she forced herself not to look around as she made for the front doors.

Alec had given her explicit instructions. "A tail will be on the lookout for any suspicious behavior. If you were really taking an animal into a shelter, you wouldn't be worried about who might be watching you, following you or anything else for that matter. You'd be focused on getting the animal inside. Once you're in, you can glance at anyone in the lobby, but don't do more than that. Walk straight past the front desk, act as if you own the place and hope like hell you're not stopped."

She got in the front door without waking Allie and did precisely as Alec had told her to do. She couldn't tell if either of the two people waiting in the lobby were FBI agents or not.

"We'll be back for her," Alec had said. His jaw had been clenched and the rigid set of his features had lent the words the flavor of a desperate vow. She clung to that single phrase as she rounded the reception desk, thankfully unmanned, and made for the back offices.

Now, inside their destination, she had to fight an urge to keep walking, straight through the building and on out the back door, carrying her baby with her, escaping the danger, the fear, by just running and running and never looking back. And she warred against a need to pull Allie out of the pet carrier and hold her tightly to her breast, to grip her little girl with all the ferocity of a wild animal fearful of losing its young.

In the end, she only turned left at the end of the hall and carried Allie through the doorway leading to the kennels, narrowing her nostrils against the ammonia odors and trying to close her ears to the raucous call of forty or fifty excited dogs and cats. She was so focused on not falling apart, on keeping things together, she almost walked right past her aunt Margaret.

"Oh, my God, Cait, I've been worried to death!"

Cait's aunt Margaret looked so much like her that Alec knew he could have picked her out of a hundred other fifty-six-year-old women standing in a fluorescent-lighted animal shelter obviously guarding the door against intruders.

"I'm afraid you'll have to wait in the lobby, sir," she said firmly. "Unleashed animals aren't allowed in this section of the shelter."

Alec's lips twitched at her clever put-down. "I'm Alec MacLaine."

She eyed him up and down before stepping back and allowing him through the doorway into a small cubbyhole of an office. Cait, different but still as beautiful in her strange hair, sat in a chair in the corner of the room, hugging Allie and rocking her a little.

Cait's eyes were shut and tears seeped from beneath her lids. Ah, what had he done? Because he'd so needed to see her, he'd placed her life in the gravest of danger.

"You're thorough. I doubt most people would have thought of bringing a dog to a shelter as a cover," Aunt Margaret said.

"It's a toy." He handed it to her.

"How clever. Looks like the real thing. Probably brighter, though. Lhasas are notoriously sweet and shockingly stupid." She petted the toy before setting it down on the square, shabby desk. Turning back to him, she held out her hand. "Margaret McBride."

"Thanks for doing this," he said, taking her hand, liking her firm grip, her cool touch.

Aunt Margaret gave him an odd look, then closed the door, shutting out most of the animals' cries. Alec thought her office smelled like the rest of the place—that combination of animal fear, wet hair, cat and dog food, and something medicinal.

Aunt Margaret moved beside Cait in a clearly protective stance, but her eyes were on the man accompanying her niece. "You look remarkably healthy for a dead man," she said coolly.

He didn't try pretending he'd misunderstood her comment; she was clearly asking why he had let Cait believe him dead for two years. "I thought Cait was dead, Ms. McBride. I came to Washington the minute I found out she wasn't. Unfortunately, some people seem to want me to really *be* dead. And they followed me to Cait's.''

He decided an FBI interrogator couldn't have looked more skeptical than Cait's aunt. She scrutinized him carefully, and he was reminded of Allie's first good look at him. Like his daughter, Aunt Margaret didn't smile, nor did she frown. After a few seconds she turned her head, and Alec had the feeling that he'd survived some test. Not passed it, necessarily, just made it through alive.

"You're bringing them to me for safety?" she asked.

"Just Allie," Cait said.

Margaret McBride pursed her lips over this, then shook her head. "No. I'm not letting you go with him, Cait."

Cait smiled faintly, apparently at her aunt's parental tone. "I have to, Aunt Margaret." Her eyes were free from tears now, though her face was still wet and shiny. "They can get to Alec through me."

"It's more than that," Alec said. "If she's spotted, they wouldn't believe she didn't know where I was."

"The police?"

"It's the FBI that's after us, Aunt Margaret," Cait said. She shifted a waking Allie to her lap. "But they won't believe Allie would know anything."

"Kitties?" Allie asked, accurately judging the scents in the small office. "Kitties, here?"

"In a minute, darling," Aunt Margaret said. "And me? Why wouldn't the FBI believe I wouldn't know where you are?"

Alec answered. "Because they're not going to know we've been here. And they're not going to know you have Allie with you."

"I'm a reasonably bright woman, Mr. MacLaine—"

"Alec."

She nodded in his direction, though she didn't use his name. "It taxes my imagination to see how I could keep a baby hidden away forever."

Alec didn't wince at her implication that they wouldn't be coming back, though it flayed him to the quick. "You won't have to. If all goes well, it'll be a few days. Tops." He outlined their swiftly concocted plan utilizing the pet carrier and told her what to look out for in the way of bugging devices and how to neutralize surveillance toys.

She looked from him to Cait. "Keep curtains drawn. Look for different knobs on my lamps and electronics. Television going all the time. Taped animal sounds. All right, I can do all that. My neighbors will think I've gone completely round the bend, but then, that'd be nothing new. But I still don't see why Cait has to go with you. We could use the same ploy with her."

"I won't fit in a pet carrier," Cait said. As an attempt at humor, Alec thought it fell sadly flat, but he felt she deserved a Medal of Honor for trying.

"We could use some other ruse," Aunt Margaret offered. "I have friends visiting all the time."

Alec didn't have to say the words, and was relieved when Aunt Margaret sighed. "I know, I know, it would look a little too convenient, my having a young friend come stay with me right at the time my niece disappears. And not a soul I know would think anything of my carrying one more dog or cat into my menagerie."

No one said anything for a moment, then Alec said gently, "We have to go, Cait." He ached to have more time with Allie himself and knew saying goodbye must be killing Cait. But it would look odd if either of them stayed any longer; unless they worked at the animal shelter, as Aunt Margaret did, they would be far more likely to simply drop off a critter and leave. Separately, of course. He'd arrived on foot, he'd depart that way. And the tears sure to be streaming down Cait's lovely face could simply be attributed to leaving a sick or dying animal behind.

So far, their plan was working, but with each passing second his tension escalated and he found himself with his arms already loosened and his knees slightly bent, ready for action. Several times he pressed his arm to his side just to assure himself the gun was still there.

Cait rose to her feet and lifted Allie to her shoulder. "Kiss me goodbye, sweetie. You're going to stay here with Aunt Margaret for a while. And see . . . the p-puppies . . . and kitties."

"Kitties!" Allie crowed happily.

The sorrow in Cait's face was breaking Alec's heart and he was afraid it was mirrored on his own. He felt suffused with a hitherto unknown pain, a purely paternal, unfamiliar sense of his own mortality, his inability to make the world perfect for his little girl. And he felt deep and utter shame for bringing this into Cait's life. Into Allie's.

He'd promised Cait things would be all right. He'd promised her they'd be back for Allie. She'd been right to tell him he couldn't. But if ever a man would try, it would be him. Now. For Cait and Allie and Aunt Margaret. For a family he'd never thought to have, for a future Cait had made clear didn't even exist.

There might not be a future to look forward to, but he was determined to do everything in his power to set a small chunk of the world back to rights again. In a perfect world Cait wouldn't just be the mother of his child, the stranger he'd connected with two years ago—she would be his partner, his wife. And the child passing to her aunt's wise and loving arms would have his name as well as his genetic code and he would have her love, her trust.

He'd held Allie, felt her fingers on his large hands, talked with her, played with her in the course of two perfect days. He'd even changed her diaper. But he hadn't thought what it would feel like to say goodbye to her, hadn't guessed the intensity of the pain that would produce.

At Cait's moan, Alec instinctively wrapped his arm around her, clasping her sagging body into him. He knew she was unaware of him, that her entire focus was on saying goodbye without breaking down.

"I'll walk you out," Aunt Margaret said.

"No, don't!" Alec and Cait said simultaneously, although for vastly different reasons. He knew Cait's instinctive cry came from agony, an undiluted need to walk away without looking back. His own came from the knowledge that danger waited for them on the other side of the door.

"You go first, Cait. Wait for me where you dropped me off before."

Without another word, her hand over her mouth and tears freely spilling down her face, Cait grabbed the now-empty pet carrier and stumbled from the room. The sound of the door closing behind her reverberated in Alec's very soul.

"You had better take care of her, Alec MacLaine," Aunt Margaret said sternly.

"With my life," he said slowly. A promise.

She eyed him narrowly. "You had better," she said. "So go."

"Goodbye. Thanks."

She nodded.

"Bye-bye," Allie said.

"That's right." Aunt Margaret approved. "Say good-bye to Daddy."

Allie held out her arms to her father, wrapped her chubby, warm limbs around his neck and planted a large, openmouthed, wet kiss on his cheek. "Bye-bye," his daughter chirped.

Baby-soft tendrils of her hair tickled his nose. Tears pricked his eyes. "Goodbye, little one," he said hoarsely.

Chapter 13

Monday, November 12, 3:30 p.m. EST

By the time Alec walked the three blocks from the animal shelter to rejoin her, Cait had managed to quell her tears and dry her face. But the pain of leaving Allie would be marked on her and, she was sure, on Alec for a long time to come.

For the first time, in the act of handing their daughter over to Aunt Margaret for safekeeping, they had become "parents." Allie was no longer just "her" daughter, but "theirs."

She moved to the passenger side and Alec scooted the seat back so he could fit behind the steering wheel. He didn't look at her as he put the car in gear and pulled out into the sparse traffic.

"Are you hungry?" he asked before reaching the

highway that would take them back to Washington, on
to uncertainty.

"No," she answered. "I would choke."

"Me, too."

"Do you really think it'll work? That they won't suspect Allie is with Aunt Margaret?" She'd asked the
question before.

His answer was the same. "It has to." He pulled the
blond wig from his head and tossed it into the back seat.
He ran his hand through his hair.

Cait did the same and some of her tension ebbed as the
constrictive wig was discarded.

He took the car onto the highway without saying anything more. And the farther they went from Kitty Hawk,
the more comfortable Cait felt. She hadn't realized how
deeply afraid she'd been for Allie's safety. Each moment
that had passed, except for the time spent in Alec's arms,
she'd feared something happening to Allie. A stray bullet, broken glass, the trauma of witnessing her mother's
murder.

None of those things could touch her daughter now.

"Are you okay?" Alec asked. She knew the question
was purely rhetorical. She couldn't answer him honestly
and he didn't want her to.

"I'll do," she said. "And you?"

He flicked her a tight glance. "I'm fine."

She had the distinct feeling they were hiding behind lies
and banalities. She couldn't talk openly with him now,
partially because her emotions were too close to the surface, but more likely because she didn't fully understand
what, exactly, she was feeling. For a stunning moment
she longed for the communication of passion, to let her
lips and hands tell him how she hurt, how she feared the
future, how she longed for surcease from all thought.

"We have to talk, Cait," Alec said slowly.

"No," she said with some panic.

He studied the road instead of looking at her. His hands rested heavily on the steering wheel, his jaw muscle worked and belied his impassivity. "Cait..."

Her heart pounded in sudden, fearful thrums. She didn't want to hear whatever he was about to say. She tucked her cold and shaking hands between her legs, as much to control their trembling as to warm them.

"I don't want to talk," she said abruptly, uttering the raw truth, afraid of anything he might say now.

He shifted his eyes from the highway to meet her gaze squarely, directly. She felt that intimate and so very rare contact to her soul. He might as well be kissing her, running his hands over her body.

"We have to," he said roughly. He shifted his gaze and she felt a pang of regret even as she breathed deeply in abject relief. Nothing about her was cold now, but everything quivered.

"If—*when*—all this is over, I want to be a part of Allie's life. Yours and Allie's. Even your aunt Margaret's. Do you understand me, Cait?"

She understood him perfectly, but even as it shot a burst of pure adrenaline straight to her heart, she shook her head. "Which 'all this' do you mean, Alec? This particular situation with the FBI coming after you? Or you taking on another new name? Or you going undercover for another mission?"

"Assignment."

"What?"

"We call them assignments."

She felt a blast of fury work through her. "Damn you, Alec. Are you listening to me? I don't want to wake up

every day wondering if this will be your last. I don't want
to have Allie around guns. I don't want—''

He jerked the car to the side of the road and slammed
on the brakes so swiftly the Chevrolet rocked in place. He
sat staring forward for several seconds before turning his
gaze to meet hers. She felt seared to her core by the blaze
of anger in the blue depths.

Her own flare of temper died as suddenly as it had been
born and, at something he could apparently see on her
face, his faded, also. She couldn't read his expression
then, and realized with a sense of shock that *not* reading
him was the way it should be. Real people had emotions,
hidden thoughts, complex realities. Only in a fantasy
would she know his every whim, desire, need.

"I don't like what's going on, Cait," he said. "Everything in me hates it. But that doesn't change what I am.
I'm a federal agent, trained to do the very best job I can.
I carry a gun, I carry a badge, and if I have fifty other
names, I'm still the same man that held you in his arms
this morning and kissed his daughter goodbye a little
while ago."

This was all said in a quiet, utterly controlled voice. He
turned slowly, put the car back in gear and pulled out
onto the highway again. If she hadn't been staring at him,
she wouldn't have noticed that his hands were shaking
and his knuckles were pinched white.

She turned her gaze out the window, inches away from
him but feeling miles apart.

"What you want isn't real, Cait," he said finally. "You
want to know for sure that I'll walk out of your door in
the morning and come back in the evening after work,
briefcase in hand."

"Is that so much to ask?" she murmured.

"Yes, Cait. Damn it. It is. Because you're not really talking about me having a normal job. You want to know, with absolute certainty, that I won't skip out on you again."

Cait felt his words carve a deep score. She raised a trembling hand to her mouth. He was right. But he was wrong, too. "Yes, part of me wants to know exactly that. I don't understand what we meant to each other two years ago and I sure don't understand what's happening now. But I thought you were dead. There wasn't any uncertainty. Now I know you're alive. I can't go through that again."

"Well, I can't give you any guarantees, Cait. There aren't any. I could lie and patronize you, but as you told me, you don't deserve that." He looked down at his fierce grip on the steering wheel. She saw him will his fingers to loosen their hold. His lips pursed and he exhaled sharply. "But I'll be damned if I can drive another mile with a lie on my lips," he said.

He flicked on the turn signal and whipped the car down a narrow, obviously seldom-used road. Grasses brushed at the underside of the car and sand slowed the tires.

"Where are we—?"

He looked over at her, cutting her words in midquestion. He captured her gaze with the depth of his emotions. Blue fire burned in his eyes before he looked back at the track they traveled.

He said slowly, clearly, "There were too many things left unsaid two years ago, words, promises...commitments. Each one of those preyed on me, knowing I couldn't go back and tell you how much you'd touched me, how deeply you'd moved me."

The car swerved a little in the sandy road and he fought the steering wheel for a moment before getting it back under control. She could see the past and present roiling in him, and worse, the dark call of the future. Cait felt her fingers twitch with the urge to touch him, to stop this outpouring, even though a part of her craved it, needed to understand what lay between them.

He forced the car over ruts and sand until the ocean spilled gray and huge before them. No other cars, buildings or any sign of civilization threatened to interrupt their lonely trek down this road. He pulled the car up on a rise, angling it toward the ocean, while the driver's door hovered at right angles to the road he'd brought them down. Without facing her he threw the car into Park. As it rocked in the second of his abrupt halts, he stretched both arms out in front of him, gripping the steering wheel as if for life.

Still without looking at her, he said, "I know you're scared about the future, Cait. So am I. I don't know what happened between us two years ago. But whatever that something was, it was never buried when I thought you'd died."

This was more truth than Cait had wanted. "Alec—"

"I took on a new name, disappeared from the scene. I holed up in the mountains in New Mexico with nothing more than a computer and a satellite dish for company. And one thing kept me going—the thought of nailing whoever was ultimately responsible for your death. I didn't spend a few hours, a couple of weeks here and there. I had some trumped-up assignment, sure, but the truth is, I worked eight to ten hours a day, every day, seven damned days a week with only one thought on my mind—making someone pay for stealing you from me."

She closed her eyes, felt herself spinning, her heart pounding so loudly she could barely hear his next words.

"Because that's how I thought of it, Cait. I didn't think of you in a coffin somewhere. I didn't imagine my world was a darker, gloomier place without you—I *knew* it was."

She made some sound and he slowly turned to face her. His features were haggard and drawn, his eyes haunted. He held up his curled hands for her to see. "These hands, Cait. Do you have any idea how many times I could feel your silky hair in them? Could feel your lips brushing the backs of my fingers? Your hand stealing into mine?" He all but flung his hands into his lap. "And sometimes during the night I'd wake up and feel you pressed against my body, your leg over both of mine, pinning me. And God help me, I was grateful for your ghost."

Shocked that her thoughtless words had provoked this flood, Cait reached for him. He held out a hand to stop her, his jaw squared, his blue eyes tortured.

"I didn't just miss you, Cait. I ached for you. I hated you for dying on me. And hated myself for failing you. For letting you die. I blamed myself for it every single day."

He moved toward her now, his anger imperfectly banked, his eyes ablaze with emotion. "Well, I'm not going to torture myself with things left unsaid. I'm not going another mile down that damned highway without you knowing that you turn my brain to jelly and my guts to water."

He grabbed her and held her at arm's length, his hands digging into her shoulders, his grasp an odd combination of anger and desperation.

"I can't make you a promise, Cait, much as I'd kill to do so. I can't guarantee you a future, or even a tomorrow. But for God's sake, Cait, let me pretend. Whatever this feeling is—love, passion, desperation, call it whatever you like—just let me pretend it has a chance of survival.''

He hauled her to him, kissing her with angry intensity, lifting her off the seat and into his fierce, savage embrace.

She felt boneless and slack in his arms. The steering wheel dug into her back and her knee jammed against the armrest. And his words hammered in her head like so many drums all beaten at the same time, and the feel of his lips against her throat and his shuddering shoulders beneath her hands made her ashamed.

"Oh, Alec," she breathed.

He looked up at her and she could see a sheen of liquid in his eyes.

"I'm so sorry," she said.

He kissed her apology away, sealing it against her lips. His tongue gentled her mouth open and enticed her to respond. She raised violently trembling fingers to his chiseled face as she returned his kiss deeply and fully.

She'd heard far more than she could piece together and it only served to make her more confused than ever. She couldn't begin to understand her own conflicting feelings for him. His outburst made her feel guilty, though she'd suffered as greatly as he, because he'd understood what she'd refused to see: there were no promises—no guarantees existed. He could be killed as easily tomorrow in a car accident as by a bullet.

"Cait...damn it, Cait," he said, pulling back from her as if he were drowning. She didn't let him finish whatever it was he'd been about say. She swiftly lowered her lips to his in a kiss as fierce as his had been. She gripped his shoulders and pulled him closer still, moaning her understanding of his turmoil, letting him know her own.

"Ah...Cait," he groaned before sliding her sideways across the bucket seats and pressing her down onto the beige vinyl. His lips followed his hands and his mouth was liquid fire and his hands strong and sure.

They all but tore their clothes open, shedding few articles, desperate to achieve the touch of silken skin. He growled her name and she moaned, quivering beneath his roaming hands. He groaned and she arched her back to grant him even greater access.

He avidly suckled her breasts while his hands cupped her behind, raising her up to push against him. With a curse he opened the car doors, granting them more room, letting in a burst of cold, moist air before dragging her back into his arms and his fevered need.

This was no gentle reacquainting, no careful exploration. This desperate mating was a defiant denial of the time stolen from them, of farewells uttered to an infant daughter, of the uncertain future, of questions that could never be completely answered and wants and needs that could only be addressed here. Now. With the roiling ocean their only witness and the echo of their mutual passion.

There was no playful exchange, no slow seduction as he drove his fist into his jacket pocket for the wrapper of protection he'd apparently thought to secure before leaving the bag with Allie. He tore it open and donned the condom in seconds flat, somehow without ever letting go of her. He rolled her over him and lifted her to straddle him.

He held her firmly, surely, passionately as she rocked over him, onto him, sheathing his length, crying out as she felt him throbbing within her. He cupped her breasts and moved her with him, entreating her to follow him, to match him, urging her to join his primal demand for release.

As her breathing became ragged and her legs trembled so violently she could scarcely remain upright, he rolled her to her back and after studying her with raw demand, drove into her, fitting her perfectly, molding himself to her body as if nature had created him for that purpose alone.

It was a dramatic mating, as fiery and impetuous as the ocean stretching before them was cold and relentless. They were inflamed in their union, fired by their mutual need. And locked in his arms, rocking to a rhythm uniquely theirs, Cait knew the passion was all the more intense for the danger that waited. The very depths of their passion strengthened the fragile bonds between them, clarified their dreams and hopes, and stripped away a few more of the barriers that continually threatened to trip them.

She craved his thundering body against hers and rose to meet him again and again, pulling him deeper and harder into her. When he would have paused, perhaps to prolong their union, she dug her fingers into his firm buttocks and pulled sharply, holding him deep within her, not wanting him to think, just to be, crying his name, calling for him to join her, to stay with her, to take her into the cold-hot burning flames over that cliff's edge of madness.

He called her name as he suddenly became rigid, rock hard in the pain that rippled through him like a wall of fire. He shook violently, making her tremble, and he shuddered, making her plunge into the all-consuming conflagration only he could create, only they could find together.

They didn't say anything afterward, holding on to each other with nearly as fierce an exchange of grips as they had clung to each other in the height of passion. In that rare moment with passion still sending flames lapping along her legs, in her core, Cait understood so much she hadn't before.

They had never truly been alone together until this moment. Terrorists had lurked outside their bower two years before. Allie had been sleeping in the adjoining room in the motel. In this place only yards from where the ocean met the land, they regained, in the sight of nature and November-gray skies, a measure of what had been ripped from them all that time ago. They had seized a honeymoon of sorts, a single union of primal need, a time of togetherness before the battle to be waged in the days and hours to come.

And though it had begun in tangled emotion, it had ended in purification. Like the phoenix, they had met in fire and now clung together new, fresh, renewed and strangely complete in the aftermath.

No words could ever say as much.

But never were words needed as badly as right then.

Cait longed to give him the simple, beautiful phrase that would lay a foundation for the future, but to say "I love you" wasn't possible. She had a baby to think about...*his* baby. And guns, death certificates and the entire concept of being on the run didn't mesh with the reality of taking care of Allie.

When we're out of this, she longed to say, but didn't, wouldn't, because there weren't any promises, even if the next few days could possibly be mapped out in perfect harmony. They didn't know each other. Not really. The passion, yes, and the desire. But what about that host of other things, the knowledge of each other, the shared beliefs, hopes, ideals, values ... even if the danger was over, they still wouldn't know about those so very important things.

Like the cold, impersonal ocean running at the shore, they had come together, a perfect blend of two different elements, but like the stormy, mysterious body of water, they retreated from the very goal they endlessly sought.

Chapter 14

Monday, November 12, 7:45 p.m. EST

Alec took the cup of coffee Cait handed him without being able to look at her. Somehow, in the evening lamplight in their motel room, this one in Fairfax, Virginia, he found it impossible to believe he'd railed at her like a madman earlier that afternoon. He'd said so much, but not nearly enough to make the evening easy. And their lovemaking haunted him, made him feel both restless with a need to escape this hunger and ready to grab her and take her into bed again, tenderly this time, hauntingly.

He'd told himself the magic was buried and gone, but he now knew with every scrap of sweet sanity in him that it was alive. Changed, altered, different, yes, but the essence of the magic wasn't gone at all. It flared so swiftly between them that the slightest spark could set it off. And somehow he instinctively knew that this notion of magic wasn't to be confused with lust or passion. Those miraculous feelings only augmented whatever mysterious and rich emotions he held for Cait. And no matter how much she might want to deny it, hers for him.

Passion, desire, protective instinct, simple enjoyment of the way she held her coffee cup or lightly flicked the edge of the cup with her tongue, capturing a stray drop of cream, her smile, her anger, even her skittishness around him . . . all of those complex feelings and curiosities mingled together to form a nameless, amorphous whole.

And knowing this, feeling it to his very soul, how could he not steal her away, run as far and wide as they possibly could, change their names, change their lives and find a small corner of the world where they could raise Allie, care for each other, keep each other safe?

But if he did that, wouldn't each knock on the door make him blanch, make him reach for his gun, uncertain, never sure if he would open the door to madness, killers who would once again rob him of seeing her beautiful face, hearing her rich voice, touching her silken skin or drowning in the passion she inspired in him?

How could he walk away from his little girl, cruise into a future without her? He couldn't. He never would, if he could help it. He'd only just found her, only just begun to dip into that incredible well of parental love. It tore him apart to know that if something happened to him, she would forget him within a matter of days. Just hours.

And if something happened to her? Or to Cait?

He would never recover. No deflection exercise, no revengeful motivation would replace them, nothing could serve as anesthesia to that pain. There was no painkiller strong enough. But there were too many unanswered

questions between him and Cait. They had only ever been
together in times of stress and danger. They had a right
to know if they could survive in times of peace.

Cait deserved more than living in fear, and he deserved more than living in doubt. He couldn't just pack
Cait and Allie up and run from the situation any more
than he could fly without benefit of wings. After it was
all over, he told himself, there would be time to discover
if they had a chance for the future.

Together, he and Cait had already watched the evening news and discovered that police suspected foul play
in Cait's disappearance. His name was bandied about as
a possible suspect, though police seemed inclined to dis-
count a dead federal agent as a potential suspect in her
kidnapping.

When Alec started to go for a newspaper, Cait again
opened his computer and began her self-assigned task of
sifting through his years of accumulated information.
When he asked why she continued to go back over the
notes and memos he'd already ruthlessly searched, she
murmured something about still searching for a motive.

"We may not ever understand a motive," Alec said.

"I still think we have a better bargaining position if we
know *why* this whole thing has happened," she replied.

He'd handed her the laptop and, at her request, jotted
down the passwords to a few of the secret files he'd stolen from his own division. He hadn't thought about the
fact that he'd used variations of her name for the locked
files. *Cait, Caitlin. Leigh. Wilson.* All of the files relating to his search for her killers bore her name, lending
them more ominous meaning than they'd had when he
still thought she'd died two years ago.

She gave him a long, utterly perplexing look before
settling down behind the keyboard and typing in various

commands. Before he left the room, he hesitated at the door. He knew the words he wanted to say, the phrases that needed to be said. *"This afternoon I told you I didn't know what we had together, Cait. I still don't know quite. But I love you. I know that absolutely. And I believe in us. We didn't have a chance two years ago. But we do now. And if everything goes all right, I want you to take that chance with me."*

But he couldn't let the words free. Wouldn't. He'd asked her to let him pretend, but there was no pretense in what he felt for her. He pulled the door shut behind him, needing to move, needing the sharp crisp air to sting him into rational thought.

Each step across the frost-covered parking lot macadam seemed to underscore his confusion. He wanted to tell Cait he believed they had a chance together and he wanted to hear her answer that she'd be with him forever. He wanted her to nestle in his arms and promise to marry him, be his wife, his love, the mother of his children.

In the sharp, crisp air, he found himself gulping in deep breaths as if he'd been drowning and only just now popped to the surface before going back down again. He'd almost done the unforgivable. He'd almost asked her for a commitment, something he had no right to do, no matter how much her aunt might urge it or his own desire might crave it.

He'd come close to asking earlier that morning, holding her sated, warm body pressed against his, feeling the rightness of their union, feeling at that moment, in the wake of their loving, that a future was sane and possible.

But they were in danger. Desperate, life-threatening danger. Trouble that had begun more than two years ago and that had reportedly claimed both their lives once already waited for them. What kind of a man would seek a commitment from a woman when he couldn't even promise her something as simple as a tomorrow?

Hell, he couldn't even truly say he'd given her a past. He'd had to ask her to tell him about his own daughter. Hours was all they had shared, then and now. Mere hours. How could he possibly dream of asking her for a future he couldn't even define based on a few stolen hours out of a lifetime?

Hours that haunted him still. Haunted her. Because so many things had been left unsaid and undone between them. And those nebulous "things" needed time to unfold.

He couldn't promise anything, because it could all be snatched from them at a moment's notice, at the whine of a silencer, the thunder of an unexpected car veering out from a dark alley.

Restless, eager to escape his thoughts and seeking some hope of the danger's end, he bought a newspaper at the motel's front desk and flicked through the sections until he found the classifieds. These he snapped open, scanning the Personals column searching for a message from Jack.

About halfway down the third column, nestled between a plea for a single white male of no specific age, appearance or profession but needing to be a Capricorn, and a demand for a freethinking married partner into sadomasochism, he found what he was looking for. He read it through twice before refolding the newspaper and leaving the front office. And if his steps felt no lighter, he at least felt the promise of action finally about to be undertaken.

Cait glanced up at him as he opened the motel room door, letting in a blast of fresh, ice-cold air. Her lovely face, only half hidden by the laptop screen, seemed to have more color than it had had only moments before and her chin was set in a determined oval.

He found he was grateful for her absorption with the computer. He didn't want to look into her eyes and let her know that the future was already here, that the moment of confrontation was at hand; it was now or never. He shut the door and drove the dead bolt into place. He felt it was a lock on a door within his heart, a lock he'd never wanted back and now couldn't afford to lose.

"Is the message you were looking for in the paper?" she asked absently. He could have kissed her.

"Yes," he said, and pulled the classified section free of the paper.

"I suppose it's in code."

He smiled, but knew it was forced. "Naturally," he said. He read the ad aloud. "J.K. seeks willing partner in safe, protected relationship. Big free-for-all. Send immediate response to Box 1792, Vienna, Virginia. Presents and securities waiting after 10:00 p.m. Tuesday for your reply."

"Well, either your friend has a twisted sense of humor or there's a great deal hidden in that message," Cait said, peering at him over the laptop screen. "Translation, please."

"Jack's offering me a safe house for you. He's warning me that at least one of our other friends is still in the picture and is gunning for me. The box number is the address, the word *box* is the house number—you know, like the alphabet on the telephone—and the 1792 is either Columbus Drive or Ocean. Maybe Blue. It's in Vienna, at any rate. That shouldn't be hard to look up."

"And the presents and securities?" Cait asked, not looking at him now as she typed a few keys and he saw the computer screen flash as the information shifted.

Knowing Cait's dislike for guns, he hated telling her, but he'd sworn only that afternoon that he wasn't going anywhere with a lie between them. A thousand other unresolved things, yes, things like dreams, hopes and wishes. But no lies. "Presents means weapons," he said.

"And securities?" she asked.

"His promise to back me up."

"His promise," she repeated.

"That's all a man can really be judged by," Alec said slowly. She looked up and met his gaze. "His word." He didn't know why he'd laden the words with such meaning; he himself hadn't made her any promises, hadn't given his word.

She flushed slightly but didn't look away. "I see."

"I hope you do," he replied, meaning himself, the things he'd said with his touch, his kisses, promises left unspoken.

Cait nodded as if she'd agreed with him about something, then looked back down at the laptop. She scanned the screen before her then flipped to another document.

"This is a man who essentially lied to you," she said, and typed a series of keys. The computer clinked and made a whirring noise. "He didn't let you know I was alive or that you had a daughter." She looked up at him.

"I have to believe he had a good reason," Alec responded, but staring into her eyes, he honestly couldn't think of a single one to excuse the magnitude of Jack's omissions.

"Well," Cait said, leaning back in the motel's desk chair and lifting her hands to flex her fingers then cup them behind her head, "I happen to agree with you." She flashed a brilliant smile at him. "Jack's not a bad guy. And I can prove it."

"What?" He felt a shock of adrenaline course through him, both from the smile and the glint of mischief he saw in her eyes. Would she never fail to take the wind out of his sails?

"You said something this afternoon about years of knowing someone having to count for something."

"Right..."

"He was counting on you believing that when he slipped you that coded message on the news the other day and the one in the paper today, right? I mean, he knew enough about you to know you always watch the news, and if you saw him, you would very likely still trust him."

Alec nodded. He couldn't figure out where she was going, but knew instinctively it was worth the tantalizing wait.

He realized she wasn't doing this researching to alleviate her own fears, but to substantiate his faith in Jack. He felt about two times stronger than he had just seconds before.

"We've got plenty of time, then," she said.

"For what?"

"I'm assuming the time mentioned in the ad means Jack won't be there until ten, right?"

"Right," Alec said. "But what—?"

Cait held up her hand, interrupting him. "I've almost got it," she said.

"What are you working on?" he asked, crossing to stand behind her.

"Not yet."

"At least give me a hint," he said.

"Münchhausen syndrome," she muttered. "By proxy."

"What's that?"

"Baron Münchhausen was a man who ran around half the world about the time of the French Revolution telling the most outrageous stories. According to him, he single-handedly saved the day in every major battle from France to Africa."

Cait's fingers flew across the keyboard and the screen flashed with incomprehensible programming language.

"What does he have to do with the price of eggs?" Alec asked.

"They named a mental disorder after him. Münchhausen syndrome—in superlay terms—is where you have to be the center of attention in regard to a medical problem, even if you have to poison yourself to get noticed. And then there's Münchhausen syndrome by proxy."

"You give someone else attention?" Alec asked, interested despite himself.

"Not quite," Cait said, still rapidly typing in something. "Almost." She leaned back in her chair and turned her gamine face all but upside down to look at him. "I got to thinking about this after going through all your information."

"When?" Alec asked.

She actually had the audacity to tilt her head back to flash him a saucy smile. It landed somewhere beneath the belt. She went back to the screen, leaving him feeling sucker punched.

"I was also thinking about something your friend Jack said during that interview in front of my garage. Scattered among all the lies and cryptograms, I mean."

"What?" Alec asked, his shoulders stiffening up. "What did he say?"

Cait glanced up at him, literally beaming. How dared she sound so cheerful, look so happy? She was in the gravest danger a person could possibly be. "He said some informed source told the FBI that you might be responsible, in some part, for the tragic incident at the WHO."

Alec felt the frown on his forehead. "I'm sorry, Cait, I'm not—"

She interrupted him. "Then he said you might be the 'engineer' behind the incident."

Alec felt a wash of goose bumps crawl up his arms. "Oh, my God," he muttered. "Fred." He leaned across Cait to view what she'd called up on the screen. Frederick Masters's personnel records, records he himself had stolen ages ago. "I didn't even catch it."

He realized he'd had this information all along but it had taken Cait to glean the message in Jack's impromptu warning. "Fred Masters holds *two* degrees from Princeton. One in law, like most of us in the FBI, and the other in *engineering*."

"Okay," Cait said. "So Jack was trying to tell you Fred was our man. Now look at this." Her fingers flew across the keyboard and a chart appeared on the screen.

"What's this?" Alec asked. He'd never seen it before.

"Something I threw together after I found out Fred had that engineering degree," Cait told him as she thumbed the laptop's mouse button and sent the cursor streaking to the first gray-and-white column. "These are dates when the FBI was involved in an incident involving White Separatists, Aryan Nation groups, or right-wing cultists."

"And these?" Alec pointed to a darker gray column with letters neatly cataloged.

"Initials."

"Initials," he repeated slowly. And saw them. Jack's, Fred's, Jorge's, even his own. A few others from alternate divisions were included, as well. "These are the FBI agents in charge of the operations?'' he asked. At her nod, he pointed to the last column. ''And this?''

''Our engineer,'' Cait said, leaning back in the chair and smiling broadly. Discounting her smile, Alec found he liked the way she said ''our,'' as if they were a team. A real team. Maybe the notion of a commitment wasn't so very farfetched after all.

She said, ''If you'll notice, each time an incident happened, at least one month prior to that incident Fred Masters suffered a sharp reduction of personal funds.''

''How did you do this?'' he asked.

''Well, I just seem to have a head for data.''

''If you ever want a job with the FBI...'' he said.

She flashed another of her mischievous grins at him. ''Well, I do suspect there's going to be a vacancy there sometime very soon. Of course, with you coming back from the dead—''

He dropped his hands to her shoulders and shook her slightly. Playfully. And was stunned to realize how natural it felt to joke with her, play with her, all the while discussing the man who wanted him dead. Then, like a bolt of lightning, he understood what else she was implying with her quip about a vacancy. She implied a future. And realized he'd done the same. *If you ever want a job...*

People couldn't just drift in the dark, uncertain present. It was only human nature to plan, to dream. To hope in the face of insurmountable odds. His hands tightened on her shoulders and he leaned down and pressed his lips against her temple.

She smiled a little and leaned into his kiss. And pressed another key on the laptop keyboard. The screen cleared and a message appeared asking them to wait. ''You need to upgrade your memory,'' she said.

"I don't think so," he said, but he wasn't talking about the computer. She shot him a glance he couldn't read at all, but it served to wipe the grin right off his lips.

"What does that Münchhausen syndrome by proxy have to do with Fred Masters?" Alec asked.

"It's the motive, Alec. I know I'm right. It's not technically Münchhausen by proxy—I'm just using that as an example of what I think he's doing, okay? Münchhausen by proxy is an unusual disorder, albeit clinically researched. They've found the disorder in the primary or secondary caretaker of a child—usually the mother, and more often than not a mother who is a nurse or is in some way connected with the medical field. The mother actively and purposefully harms her own child. It's child abuse, of course, but not the usual run-of-the-mill beating or yelling. She might try smothering, or injecting them with something that causes a severe but fairly short-term reaction—hives, arrested breathing, something like that."

Alec couldn't help his involuntary protest.

"I know," Cait said, and he knew she was thinking about Allie. "But unfortunately, it happens. After the child nearly dies at home, the mother calls an ambulance or in some other dramatic fashion manages to get the child to the hospital where everyone can see the child's in dire trouble, but even the best doctors can't come up with a precise diagnosis. The mother's unswerving devotion, dogmatic persistence and loving, tender care seem to be the only things that save the day and finally, they go home. Only to have the child get sick again. And again."

Alec thought he understood what it was Cait was leading to, much as it sickened him to acknowledge it. He thought of the many times he'd eaten dinner at the Masters's home, of Fred's staunch loyalty to the bureau. And of Fred's often repeated conviction that something had to be done to wake the country up to the bureau's importance.

"Fred Masters is like the mother," Cait said. "The FBI, his child. Don't you see? I think he's actually creating incidents around the country, incidents that shock the nation at their violence, their complete lack of respect for peace officers, for human life. And then he quells the riots and the furor and saves the day. He's like a psychotic fireman who, incidentally, is also the arsonist who started the fire."

"The motive," Alec said. And he knew she was right. It fit, and it fit perfectly. "I never would have seen it in a million years," he said.

Her smile faltered a little. "No, because he was your friend. And you trust your friends, Alec. You don't look for the bad in your friends."

"I'm an FBI agent. That's ninety-nine percent of what we do."

"But only when you're searching for bad guys. Here you were looking for dirt on someone you cared about. You don't have it in you to look for the bad in the people you love."

He felt as if the world skipped a full beat in its rotation, throwing him off balance. What was she trying to tell him? "Are you giving me a hard time?" he asked, forcing a grin to his lips.

"No," she said seriously, starkly honest. "Someday I want you to teach Allie how to look at life the way you do."

He felt as if she'd just given him the softest little push off the tallest peak in the Grand Canyon. He would undoubtedly understand the ramifications of what she had said about the time he hit bottom.

Chapter 15

The tension in the stolen car seemed to bounce off the windows. Strangely, after all the other unusually anxious moments they'd spent together, this tension wasn't born of the past but of the future. Their future.

Alec hadn't said more than three words since getting in the car. And his stiff silence precluded any conversation from her. Not that Cait had anything to say. She'd *not* said it all in the motel room in Sterling before they had taken Allie to Aunt Margaret for safekeeping. And she'd *not* said it yesterday afternoon before loosing the floodgates of Alec's emotions. And her own.

And she'd managed not to say it all a thousand empty nights before that. All those unspoken words and unrevealed thoughts flayed her now, taunted her for her cowardice.

She felt oddly dissociated, as if part of her wasn't in this car, but still back in those motel rooms, rooms that had become the only home she and Alec had ever shared, or still further back than that, in that dreadful closet two years ago. She and Alec had faced death together once already in their unusual relationship. They'd both lost and won that time, though the winning had been blackened with lies and pain.

Motel rooms and cars that didn't belong to them, a closet in a building neither of them had worked in. Two years of mourning. And, aside from passion, the only real thing, the best thing they had in common had been secreted to North Carolina to be with her great-aunt for safekeeping. Everything about their togetherness was wrong, false, based on fear. And yet, when he touched her she could feel the raw honesty in his caresses. And when he kissed her she felt completely whole, as if part of her had been missing until now.

She thought about her conviction that they couldn't talk about a future because there wasn't any to talk about. She knew now she'd been dodging the truth. Short of being diagnosed with a terminal illness whose course was already run, everyone had a future. It was only as far away as a dream, as a thought, as a word.

With the single exception of Allie, she'd spent the entire past two years of her life avoiding anything to do with the concept of a future. In some dimly understood manner she'd known if she embraced a future, she'd have to relinquish the past. And letting go of the past meant letting go of her memories of Alec, letting go of the fantasies, the pretty illusions, the dreams.

She frowned, thinking furiously. She didn't believe the tension crippling communication could be put down solely to Alec's refusal to talk. Cait felt something else, that not-quite-right frisson of unidentifiable emotions tickling at her. One was related to Alec, to how she felt or was scared to feel about him, and the other told her danger lurked just ahead.

More than anything else, that second sensation reminded her of the night Alec had shown up on her doorstep, alive again after two years. She'd known before he ever rang her bell that things were wrong, that something was off-kilter in the world. She had that same feeling now.

Studying him, she knew he felt it, too. His eyes continuously flicked from the Lee Highway to the rearview mirror. His lips were drawn in a thin, tight line and he seemed to be clenching his teeth. He never turned his head to glance her way, yet she had the sense that he knew her every gesture, each blink of an eye.

He'd located the street—it was Ocean, not Columbus—by the simple means of borrowing the hotel desk clerk's city directory. And the word *box* translated to the number, 269, taken straight from the lettered numbers on a telephone. They knew exactly where they were going but the closer they drew to Vienna, the more nervous he seemed to become.

Vienna was less than fifteen miles away from Fairfax, but the beltway and the cruise up Route 7 made it seem shorter. The car seemed to be eating up the road, stripping them of the safety inherent in mere minutes. She wanted to yell at Alec to stop the car, to turn around, to disappear into America somewhere and forget all about the FBI, Fred Masters, Jack King. For each mile closer to the safe house they came, they grew further apart, as if the speedometer that registered the wheel's revolutions also stole, bit by bit, second by second, any chance they had of a future together.

She had stalled their departure for the safe house as long as she possibly could. But in the end, it was simply time to go. And their uncertain future was at hand. And no amount of wishing it away was possible now.

Sitting beside him, aching just to touch him, reassure herself that he was with her, in body if not in soul now, she devoutly wished they'd had those fifteen years he'd shared with Jack, the years with Fred. And she wished she could have told him yesterday afternoon, or while in his arms last night, what she really felt about him. It wasn't illusion or fantasy. What she felt, even if she didn't fully understand then or now, was real, however confused, and he had a right to know about her feelings for him.

When loading their bags into the car, he'd taken extra care not to brush her fingertips, nearly dropping one of the suitcases in his efforts to avoid touching her, as if mere contact would scorch him.

Twice since then she'd caught him watching her via reflections in the mirror or the windshield. But she couldn't break through that rigid control of his. Couldn't make him give a single inch. Or was his fierce self-control a mirror of her own? Wasn't it really her that wouldn't give in, wouldn't allow the possibility of a future?

It was her denial of the future, her refusal to accept even the glimmer of a future that stripped hope and dreams from the present. And it was her shying away from the all too nebulous "ever after" that sat between them like a palpable third presence. A very large and daunting presence.

Cait's mind seemed to revolve with each cycle of the wheels on the pavement. Each leafless tree they passed, every sprawling and frost-covered farmhouse that leapt out and disappeared as the car whizzed down the highway seemed to sharpen her acuity, heighten her perceptions.

He'd sworn there would be no lies between them. He'd sworn it and she instinctively believed he'd held to his word. *Sometimes that's all a man can offer.* He hadn't lied to her, nor had she lied to him. But by leaving out the promise of any future together, they'd done worse. They'd stripped all beauty from the world, stolen all hope.

But worse than any lies, past or present, she was allowing the silence to write the future for them. She would be safely stashed away while he went to battle. For her.

What if she didn't say anything and he never came back to her? What if...?

"Damn," Alec muttered. He wiped his mouth with the back of his hand, as though he'd felt a blow delivered.

"What is it?" she asked.

"I love you, Cait."

His words pierced her like a rapier through the heart.

"It's unfair. I can't even promise you a live ending, let alone a happy one."

She didn't say anything, somehow knowing he wasn't finished.

"But I had to tell you. I can't go into this without letting you know," he said slowly, deliberately.

With his uncomfortable ability to think along the same lines, he'd unknowingly pierced the core of her greatest fear. Cait felt cold and hot at the same time. Life wasn't a fairy tale, she wanted to tell him. An ending with both

Code Name: Daddy

of them alive was enough. Living together was a huge next step and living together happily ever after was so far removed from the realm of possibility that she couldn't even consider it.

"Are you afraid to say the words, Cait?" he asked softly.

Yes, she thought. She was more than afraid; she was terrified. But not of saying three simple words, difficult as that would be. She was afraid to mean them. Because if she let them out of her lips and she *meant* what she said, then losing Alec would kill her this time.

Until he'd spoken, she'd been afraid that not saying anything would haunt her until her dying day—which was all too likely to be soon, if Fred Masters got his way—but now she knew that saying them, meaning them, knowing she would always and forever mean them, would haunt her far more surely than the lack would do. Some things were better left unsaid, some gardens better left untended.

Because someday, if not today, some tomorrow or even next week, something *would* happen to him. While he was every inch the FBI professional driving the car, taking her to a safe house, he was also a statistic in one of her many computer constructs: peace officers didn't have a high rating in the long-term survival department. And an agent—no matter that the agent was loving, kind, a father, the only man who could bring her to that cliff's edge of blissful madness—was still an instrument of the law.

"I don't know what *to* say, Alec," she murmured finally, aware she was letting him down, aware she wasn't being honest with him.

"I promise you—" he began, but she stopped him by simply covering his mouth with her fingers. Alec's whole body jerked as if a jolt of electrical current pulsed through him. But he didn't turn his head or say a word.

"Please don't, Alec. You can't make promises and I can't bear to hear you try. It hurts both of us," she said sadly, and dropped her hand back to her lap. Her heart pounded so fiercely, so rapidly she could barely breathe.

"You're wrong, Cait," he said. "And if it takes me a lifetime, I'm going to prove it to you."

Cait looked out the window, unwilling to see the determination she knew would rest on his face. He was talking about a lifetime that could be measured in minutes.

Cait knew she should say something to him right at that moment. In days of old, ladies saw their men off to battle with the evidence of their love gaily fastened to their men's armor. The scarves made the men brave and strong. Words could do that, too. But she couldn't. She didn't know how. Was it because her parents had been killed when she was so young that she'd never quite learned to accept death as a fact and not abandonment? Or had she learned that more recently, when she was told that Alec had perished?

"We're here," he announced, turning the car into the Vienna subdivision entrance.

Cait's heart beat so rapidly she felt certain she would faint. The blood pounding in her ears blocked her hearing and clogged her throat. As Alec turned the car onto Ocean Street, she realized her moment to speak had come and gone. Again she'd allowed fear and doubt to steal the words from her, or more accurately, to steal them from Alec.

He slowed the car, as if reluctant to approach the safe house.

"Alec, I—"

"There it is," he said, interrupting her again.

"I need to—"

"Here's the plan," he interrupted for the third time. "I approach the house first, and if all is clear, you'll join me. But not until I wave you in. Are you with me?"

The so-called safe house looked like any other split-level, attractive home in the neighborhood. A low pine hedge, in need of some trimming, flanked two sides of the place, while a stand of tall oaks offered protection and shadows to the back. The front lawn, white with November frost, stretched from the front empty flower beds to the curb at the street.

No cars were parked out front or in the driveway.

"I don't like it," Alec said on the second pass by the house, pointing at the darkened porch. "A light should be on. Signaling an all's well." Instead, it was dark, shadowed and menacing in its absence.

Cait's skin tightened and gooseflesh rose on her arms as Alec pulled the car to an idling stop across the street from the house.

She could see that the curtains in the house were half open, but the street lamps reflected on the windows didn't reveal what waited for them inside.

"Okay. No arguments, Cait. You get in the driver's seat. I'm going to the door. At the least sign, and I mean *least* sign of trouble, you stomp on the gas and get out of here."

"Define trouble," Cait said, but she did as he asked, sliding across the seat and fumbling to shift the whole thing forward so her feet would reach the pedals.

Alec's eyebrows rose as he leaned in the door to help her. "Trouble is anything that doesn't look right. Like someone shooting me as I ring the doorbell, somebody conking me on the head, the house blowing up. Things like that."

She could see he wished he could have taken the words back the second he uttered them, as her face had blanched while she pictured each and every one of those horrific events taking place.

"Hey, hey, Cait . . . I was just kidding."

"It wasn't funny," she said, but she tried conjuring up a smile, anyway. It must have worked; he pressed a swift kiss to her cold cheek.

He started to turn away to walk to the house. She called him back. "Alec!"

For all his fears for her, she saw that most of his attention was already on the house across the street. And in a blinding flash of understanding Cait realized that a part of him was actually enjoying the moment, was wholly prepared and geared for trouble. This was his job. His profession. And he was good at it.

And she, like a million other women every day, in every town across the country, would let him do it. Bizarre as it seemed, she'd driven him to work, kissed him goodbye, fussed over him, and was now waiting for him to do his job and come back to her.

But she wasn't like a million other women and Alec wasn't her husband and she wasn't going to let him walk across that street without hearing what she had to say.

"What is it?" he asked somewhat impatiently, his eyes on the front porch light.

"C-come back to me, Alec," she blurted out. It wasn't what she'd meant to say, but the words came straight from her heart. The deepest, rawest part of her heart.

He smiled then, a crooked, I'll-be-damned grin that nearly broke her heart. And terrified her. What if something *did* go wrong? What if she never saw him again?

"I promise," he said, and she realized that on some scarcely understood level her inept words had been exactly the right ones. They were words of the future, words that defied a negative conclusion to whatever might happen inside that house.

He gave her one long last look and turned to the other side of the street.

Before she could say anything else he was already halfway up the sidewalk, his hand behind him, tucked inside his jacket, undoubtedly around the handle of his gun.

And while her heart pounded painfully in her chest, she understood at that moment, with total and blinding clarity, that Alec was no stranger, had never been one. She'd known him from the very first second she ever saw him. His life, his job, even her fantasies about him, none of those were obstacles to their happiness. Not understanding him, not trusting him with every fiber of her being, that constituted the uncrossable, unbreachable chasm.

Part of her wanted to call out to him, to bring him back long enough for her to spill this new awareness into his ears. But she had to trust him, had to trust her new-found understanding of him. She had to hold on to the memory of the way he played with Allie, the laughter in his incredible blue eyes, and even the gun that he casually tucked on top of a cabinet to keep out of Allie's

sticky reach, for it was as much a part of him as his smile
or his touch.

And if she already knew Alec, if trust was a given, then
the future wasn't a blank, nor was it something that could
be analyzed, picked apart and studied. It couldn't be
prescribed, planned, as carefully constructed as one of
her software programs. But like the data contained within
one of her programs, they had all they would need for a
future together: dreams, passion, wishes, goals. A future, any future, was only the combined aspirations and
hopes of a lifetime.

That's what she'd wanted to say when she'd told him
to come back to her, that she would try to believe in a
future with him.

And watching him go away from her, walking into
danger for her, she knew she'd never wanted anything so
much in her whole life.

Alec pressed the doorbell and tensed, waiting for the
door to swing open. The chimes rang through the house,
lending the place an abandoned air, as if it weren't merely
empty, but sadly wanting. He glanced up at the dark
porch light. Something was wrong.

He started off the porch, ostensibly to search for a key
beneath a flowerpot or doormat, and froze when he
heard the rattle of locks being drawn. This, too, wasn't
the usual setup.

He glanced from the car to the door and half turned,
slipping his gun into his belt and keeping his hands at his
hips, openly displaying his chest . . . and his seeming lack
of weapon.

From the gloom inside, dark there as well, Jack pushed
the storm door open. "Good God, Al," he said, "It's

good to see you! Damned good. You got my message, then. I was afraid you wouldn't be able to engineer your way here.''

Alec hadn't needed the full phrasing to know that everything was glaringly wrong. In any normal safe house operation, Jack would have met him outside for a quiet conference; he would never have held the door ajar. Secondly, Jack never called him Al; nobody in his right mind ever had. And thirdly, he'd used the word *engineer.*

"What's wrong with the porch light, Jackie?" Alec asked, letting his old pal know that he'd caught the references.

"Something's wrong with it. Keeps going out."

Translation: Fred Masters wasn't in the house with Jack. But was somewhere nearby. Probably watching the two of them. A shot of fear raced the adrenaline coursing through his system at the thought of Cait alone in the car. What if Fred had anticipated him leaving the car first?

Another part of his mind was working on an allusion to toss up to Jack, something that would allow him to question and answer covertly.

Jack beat him to the punch. "I don't recognize the car."

Dear God. Fred was at the car. Fear for Cait swamped his mind, driving out all logical, professional reactions. He wanted to bound across the street and empty his gun into Fred's damnable face. If he hurt so much as one hair on Cait's head, he'd kill him and damn the consequences.

But right now he didn't dare turn around, didn't dare call out a warning. Fred was as crazy as a loon. He couldn't trust him not to start shooting in the middle of a suburban neighborhood. And the one he'd be shooting was Cait.

His Cait.

He thought about his promise.

He thought about his daughter.

And he thought about all the millions of things he hadn't told Cait, things he wanted to give her, promises he needed to keep.

Fred would attack Cait if he saw Alec or Jack doing anything but standing there talking.

Cait would drive away if she heard gunfire.

Was that the answer?

Alec shifted slightly, surreptitiously drawing his gun and laying it against his thigh, pointing at the ground. He circled his finger around the trigger.

Cait put her foot on the brake. Surely whatever Alec had to say to Jack King about the past could have waited until they were all safely inside the house and out of the cold. Something was wrong. Her nerves all but jangled with the urge to flee, the need to rush out of the car and into Alec's arms.

Even in the gloom she could see Jack King's pale, pasty face. His dark eyes glittered in the doorway of the safe house that seemed anything but safe. He wasn't looking at Alec but at her. Then up the street, then back at her, then again up the street.

Alec's broad shoulders were as stiff as concrete and even from that distance and despite the darkness she could see that muscle in his strong jaw leaping as he clenched his teeth together. He flexed slightly and she saw the tip of his gun peek out on the right side of his jacket.

She knew no one else, even someone watching him closely, would have seen the gun. No one but her, because she was utterly focused on his every movement, waiting for a signal. She felt her entire life depended on noticing each stray detail.

This wasn't a time to search the memory banks of her mind and select the correct option; she knew relying on pure instinct would offer her the only viable solution. Without taking her eyes from Alec and without thinking about the ramifications of what she did, she threw the car into Park and slammed the heel of her hand on the horn.

It blared into the night like Gabriel's horn. Long, loud, shocking, it was a trumpeter's trumpet of an alarm, a magnificent, defiant call to arms.

As she'd known he would, Alec whirled, his gun stretched at right angles to his rigid body. She could see his wide eyes scanning her, the car, the bushes flanking the stolen car. He lifted the gun the merest fraction and fired into the air.

She heard the report of the gun over the loud blare of the horn and jerked her hand from the center of the steering wheel.

Alec fired again and she understood his meaning: *Get going!*

But she couldn't. Someday, she hoped he'd understand. Even if she couldn't do anything to help, she couldn't leave him.

Alec started running across the street, followed by Jack King. Was King chasing Alec or supporting him? Cait couldn't tell.

"Hold it right there, Fred!" Alec yelled. "It's over!"

Suddenly someone wrenched the passenger door open and she felt blinded by the interior lights. Even as she turned her head to see a pair of maddened brown eyes, she felt something hard and cold strike her just above the temple. Lights flashed and flickered and incredibly, everything grew dim and soft. Almost peacefully quiet.

There was something she needed to tell Alec. Something about the future. She closed her eyes, needing to think, needing to rest for a moment, trying to remember what it was she hadn't told him.

"Oh, God," said a voice in the car with her. "You weren't supposed to be involved in the first place, lady. Why the hell are you always in the wrong place."

Cait focused on the madman's rambling.

"I didn't want to kill you, you know?" he said, making his words a question, as if asking her permission.

Alec called from outside the car. "Fred! Give it up! You can't get away with this. Jack and I are both here, Fred. We'll see you get some help. Let her go."

"I can't," Fred said.

"No," Cait agreed. "It's really dark in here." That wasn't what she'd meant to say. But she couldn't think what she was supposed to do. Something about putting the car in gear and driving off, leaving Alec behind. If only her head didn't hurt so much.

"Please, Fred," Alec called out. "Don't hurt her!"

Cait blinked several times, trying to clear the strangely bobbing lights from her eyes. She reached out and grasped the steering wheel to keep from slumping to the seat.

"Don't move," Fred said.

"It was you," Cait said. "*You* killed those men."

"I didn't kill you," Fred replied heatedly. "You should have thanked me for that. I'm a federal agent, for Christ's sake!"

Cait clung to the steering wheel as if for dear life. She weaved on the seat, hanging her head down but seeing clearly now for the first time in several seconds. The gearshift knob was only inches below her right hand. Her foot was already against the accelerator.

"I killed the terrorists. That's my job. Besides, they didn't deserve to live."

She managed to cock her head just enough to see Alec's rigid form outside the car. His gun looked enormous held in front of him like that, but she felt an immense relief that the barrel was trained on Fred.

Alec called out again, as desperately as before, but the message far different.

"Don't kill her, Fred. Don't hurt the mother of my child. Please, Fred."

Fred jerked beside her as if Alec had shot him with bullets, not words. "Alec's baby?" He grabbed her chin and wrenched her to face him. "Is this true? Oh, God, is it true?"

Cait didn't know what she'd expected to see in Fred Masters's eyes—madness, or an anger so deep it would border on lunacy?—but what she saw made her feel confused. He looked in pain, more confused than she, as if by looking into her eyes and seeing the truth about Allie, about Alec, he'd learned that his entire life had no meaning, that all he was and had been had proved insignificant and futile.

"Fred—!"

Fred jerked again, his fingers tightening on her chin, but this time he didn't appear chagrined or horrified at the call, but galvanized into manic action. He twisted Cait's face toward the driver's window and yelled, "Shut up, Alec! Just shut up! I need to think! I can't think with you yelling all the time. You were supposed to die in the WHO that day. You aren't supposed to be here. When I found out you hadn't died, I decided to let you live—as long as you kept hidden away. But then you had to come looking for *her!* Damn you!''

Alec could see that Fred was shaking with the fury of his tirade. His own heart jolted sharply when his former friend viciously pressed Cait's face against the cold glass of the driver's window. Her eyes were wide, shocked, and her lips were smashed against the glass in a parody of a kiss.

He'd be damned if this was how he'd have to remember her.

''And it's against the rules to fraternize with the hostages, Alec! You aren't a rookie anymore. I can't keep going around after you cleaning up your messes!'' Fred called out.

Cait had been right; there was probably another name for whatever disorder Fred suffered, a name other than Münchhausen syndrome by proxy, but if the name signified stark raving crazy, then it fitted Fred to a *T.*

Alec tried not to think what Cait might be feeling, tried only to think how he might extricate her from Fred's terrible grip. He didn't dare look around to see what Jack was up to; he only knew his longtime partner had disappeared from even peripheral view.

''You young punks come spilling into the bureau fresh out of law school thinking you know everything about the criminal mind. You don't know anything!'' Fred yelled.

It wasn't Fred's words that made Alec's guts turn to jelly, it was the sight of Cait's slender hand inching for the gearshift knob.

"I know enough not to orchestrate murder!" Alec called out, forcing Fred's attention.

Fred all but screamed at him that he was only doing what had been necessary. "No one was giving us any credit for anything!" he yelled. "Somebody had to do something to call attention to the bureau. To let them know we're there. That they need us, damn it!"

Cait's fingers reached the gearshift and Fred half turned to see what caused her movement. As he yelled something, Alec fired his gun just inches above the car.

Before the echo of the shot faded, Fred whirled to face him, screaming something, and smacked Cait's face against the window as he fired through it at Alec.

"No!" he heard Cait scream as he heard the shot, heard the shattering of glass and felt Fred's bullet slam into his shoulder.

Despite his wide-legged stance, the slam spun Alec around and knocked him flat on his back. His arm hurt like hell and he felt winded both by the extreme tension and his fear for Cait. He rolled to his side, struggling to regain his stance.

Just as he managed to get semierect, he saw the passenger door suddenly flung open, and the interior of the car was flooded with light. Jack's body blocked exit.

Cait screamed again as Alec called out "No, Jack!" even as Fred turned and fired point-blank at Jack's broad chest.

Still screaming, Cait nevertheless seized the opportunity to crank the gearshift to the right. The car jolted backward then shot forward with a squeal of tires.

Alec yelled her name and lunged after the car. He heard her scream something, his name perhaps, and then heard a shot ring out inside the car.

"Oh, God, no!" he cried, staggering after the car. When it came to a dead halt right in front of him, he literally ran into it, sliding up over the trunk and off the back window. He rolled to the pavement and was on his feet again, unaware of the pain, unaware of anything except Cait.

He'd heard her die once, screaming his name only to stop after the first execution-style shot. It hadn't been true then. Please, God, don't let it be true now. Please, please...

He was unaware he was murmuring the words aloud as he reached the driver's door, a supplication from his heart, from his very soul.

"Oh, please, be all right, Cait, please be all right...."

Uncaring if Fred waited for him inside, he dragged open the door of the battered, stolen car and sank to his knees at the sight of Cait's slender form slumped over the steering wheel.

Fred Masters was half in, half out of the car, blood streaming down his face. Alec couldn't tell whether he was dead or alive and didn't give a damn.

"Cait...?" Alec whispered, his fear choking his voice.

When she didn't move, he loosed a yell of unvarnished agony.

And she jumped as if he'd shot her.

She turned disbelieving eyes on him.

"I s-saw you s-shot," she stammered, choking back a sob.

"Nothing to worry about," he said. "Just a scratch."

He didn't know why that made her laugh then suddenly burst into tears.

Alec wanted to draw her into his arms then and there but he had to check on Fred. And on Jack.

"Are you hurt?" he asked, pushing awkwardly to his feet.

She shook her head. "I don't think so."

"Stay there," he ordered, rounding the car, keeping his eyes and his gun trained on Fred's sprawled form. It didn't take long to know the truth: Fred Masters wouldn't be playing God with agents' lives any longer.

About ten yards behind the car Jack King lay on his side well into someone's frost-covered front lawn. Lights were going on all up and down the street and a couple of men were hovering on their porches, well within reach of their doors.

"What's going on?" one of them called.

Alec ignored them as he knelt beside his longtime friend.

"Jack?"

"Yeah," Jack breathed.

"Somebody call an ambulance," Alec called out. "Officer down!"

He heard at least two doors screech open and slam shut. "Hang on, Jack," he said, shrugging out of his jacket to make a pillow for the other man.

"I'm sorry, Alec. I should have told you a long time ago."

"Don't worry about it now."

"No. I was only trying to keep you safe."

"It's okay."

"Is she okay?"

"She's fine," Alec said, and truly realized it at that moment. His knees shook so badly he dropped to sit beside Jack. He felt for Jack's chest wound.

"Here." Some cloth was pressed into his hands. He looked up to see Cait holding out a clean disposable diaper. "Maybe this'll help."

A chuckle rippled through him as he made a bandage of the thick, padded diaper. He pressed it against Jack's wound. "Maybe guns and diapers can mix," he said, then was afraid to look up at her.

"I love you, Alec," she said and sat down beside him and leaned her head on his good shoulder. "Bullet holes and all."

Chapter 16

"What I want to know is why you started laughing when I told you it was just a scratch?" Alec asked Cait, pulling her against his chest.

"There's not enough room on this bed," she said. "Especially when you have it at this angle."

"I like it this way. All the better to—"

"Visiting hours are over in fifteen minutes," a nurse's aide said from the doorway.

"Thank you," Cait said, slipping out of his reach and back onto the floor. She straightened her blouse and assumed a prim air. "You're supposed to be convalescing."

"I told you there wasn't anything wrong with me but a— Why does that make you smile every single time?"

Her face grew serious. "Before...when I thought you were dead ... I used to imagine that someone would tell me you weren't dead, that it was nothing. What? Alec? Heavens, no. Just a scratch."

Alec didn't know what to say, so said the obvious. "Well, this time it was."

"It wasn't, either," she said with some heat. "Fred Masters managed to shoot you right where you were shot last time. Time before last, I mean."

Alec grinned. He liked the game way she was attempting to deal with the idea that bullets really did fly in his business.

"Have you ever been to New Mexico, Cait?"

"No, why?"

"Well, I have a cabin out there, you see? And I just left my assignment hanging—"

"Another assignment? Already?"

Alec couldn't help grinning at the look of horror on her face. "It's all right, Cait. I've retired my second badge."

Her features flattened a little and he didn't know what that meant. "What's wrong?" he asked.

"Are you doing this because of what I said about guns and Allie?"

She wasn't the kind of woman a man lied to. "Not entirely," he said, then grinned again. "It was what you said about loving me, bullet holes and all. Being in the hospital too often would make me lose too much time with you."

The look on her face reminded him of her aunt Margaret's scrutiny. And Allie's. "Are you serious?" she asked.

"I am."

"You'll miss it," she warned.

"I won't."

"You'll get bored and crabby and you'll want to go out every night and shoot pool."

He chuckled. "I love you, Cait." He held on to her gaze for several seconds, letting her see he was deadly serious.

"But, Alec, you love the bureau," she protested.

"You're right, Cait. I do. And I know it would work out so I could still be with the bureau and with you and Allie. But I don't want that."

"It *is* because of what I said."

"It's because I want to get to know you, Cait. Everything about you. The way you look in the morning, the expression on your face when you watch a movie, the mood swings you get when you're pregnant. All of it. The whole picture. And I can't do that gallivanting around the country on field assignments."

"But—"

"I've already missed two years, Cait. I missed my daughter's whole life. I want us to make up that time we lost. And I want to get to know Allie. Be a family. And I don't think I could go into a dangerous situation again without worrying about what would happen to you two."

She didn't have to say her thoughts; they were clear. "You won't be unhappy?"

"Only if you and Allie aren't with me." He crooked his finger at her and she stepped closer. He pulled her to him and kissed her fully, soundly and with all the promise of a future.

"What about Jack?" she said a little breathlessly when she finally broke free.

"What about him?" Alec asked, the grin wiped from his face.

"I wish you'd talk to him," she said. "He did save our lives."

Cait had been hectoring him to visit Jack every day of the week he'd spent in the hospital. He trusted his old friend, had even placed all their lives in his hands. They had worked with the precision of long-standing partners to try taking Fred Masters down peacefully. But Alec couldn't seem to forgive Jack for the time he'd stolen from them. For the fourteen months he'd missed of Allie's life.

"He's better," she said. "He's still got a long way to go, but he'll pull through."

Alec could have told Cait that much. Jack was a scrapper. "It'll give him time to do something about that ulcer. What about Aunt Margaret? Did she finally go back home?" Alec asked, thinking he truly liked Cait's aunt, though he found he felt a bit exhausted by her.

A strange look crossed Cait's face. "Not yet."

"Something wrong?"

"No."

"But something's up."

"I don't know yet," she said. She climbed back up on the bed and faced him squarely. "But if what I think is true, you're going to have to patch things up with Jack."

Alec narrowed his eyes at her. Light dawned. "Aunt Margaret?"

"She's 'Margaret' to Jack."

"You're kidding me," he said. Cait shook her head. Alec couldn't help smiling. Really, genuinely smiling. "Aunt Margaret and Jack?"

"Margaret and Jack." Cait was smiling now, too. "So, you'll talk to him?"

"Oh, I guess so."

She hopped down, only to propel the wheelchair to the side of the bed.

"Hey! I didn't mean now!"

She held out her hand. "Like you said, the sooner the better."

"Well, I'm not going to go see him in *that* thing."

A few minutes and what seemed like twelve hospital corridor miles later, he stepped around the bulky doorway of Jack's room. Margaret, who was sitting in an easy chair beside Jack's bed, raised her eyebrows when she saw Alec, and released Jack's hand to push to her feet.

"I think I'll go fetch a cup of tea," she said, beaming at Alec.

He moved aside to let her pass.

"Go easy on him," she murmured before leaving the room.

It irritated him that everyone seemed to assume he would tear Jack's head off. Not that he wouldn't if his old friend were standing, but as it was . . .

"Alec."

"Jack."

"How's the shoulder?"

"Fine. How's the chest?"

"Still ticking."

"And the ulcer?"

"Better."

"So," Alec began. He was uncomfortable with the sheer intensity of emotion he felt for this short, gray-haired, lying former partner of his.

Jack said, "So, Cait said she thought you'd eventually talk to me."

"I'm in the room."

Jack looked around him as if surprised to find that was true. "Good thing you're not armed."

"You got that right," Alec agreed, but he found he was fighting back a smile.

"Cait said I should just shoot straight. Tell you like it is."

"That would be different," Alec retorted, not feeling quite as friendly now that they were nearing the source of their problem.

"On the last assignment I went on in Nevada—the one right before your deal at the WHO—I got to talking with some of the guys who'd worked the operation in Michigan. Remember that one?"

"Sure," Alec said, knowing Jack referred to an incident with a right-wing separatist group that had resulted in one agent down, two cultists dead and six more in prison.

"One of the guys on my team mentioned that a cultist member said they'd been paid by the FBI to create a ruckus. My man swore those were the guy's exact words."

"And?" Alec prodded, beginning to see where Jack was going.

"And when I got back from Nevada, I started doing some digging. I guess you pretty much came up with the same stuff I did. Orders for incidents were coming right from our own division."

"You found it out a lot sooner than I did."

"I had a tip," Jack said.

"And you didn't want to share your information with anyone?" Alec asked. "Me, for instance?"

"Not when I knew it was coming from someone in our own division."

"Meaning you thought I was involved."

"No. Hell, I didn't think that, Alec."

"Sure you did, Jack. That's why you told me to play dead and take on a new identity. Why you let me believe Cait was dead. You wanted me safely hidden away."

"I knew you weren't involved when you got shot, damn it. And I knew it was pretty good odds you'd been marked for death. That narrowed my list of suspects to Fred or Jorge, and that seemed as far out as you being involved."

"Hell, Jack, I can't beat you up over thinking I was in on it. I thought the same thing about you. There were only four of us. And I knew it wasn't me."

"And when you learned Cait Wilson was still alive—"

"Yeah."

"I was having you watched, in case Fred or Jorge tried anything again. And you slipped them when you came to Washington. If you'd hung around to talk to me that night, a lot of this could have been avoided."

"If you'd just let me in on it, *all* of it could have been."

Jack shrugged. "Who can say?"

"One question. Who was waiting for me at Cait's house that night?"

"Fred. I'd put the word out to take you out of harm's way. It never occurred to me that if I could keep tabs on you, someone could also keep tabs on me. He outfoxed the fox.

"Fred was crazy. I didn't even guess that. Did you?" Jack asked.

"No. Not until Cait came up with a motive."

"Yeah. Pretty weird stuff, huh?"

"It's bad press for the bureau," Alec said.

"You had to do it. Maybe there's too much secrecy in this business." Jack gave him a funny look. "Are you done raking me over the coals?"

"Yeah."

"Then tell me, how many cars did you steal, anyway? You're a regular one-man crime wave."

Alec told him and they both started laughing.

Epilogue

Thursday, November 21, 3:30 p.m. MST
One year later

"Pinecone," Allie said, holding up another of her finds. It was the fiftieth one she'd handed Alec during their short walk from the cabin. All of his pockets were bulging and his arms were filled.

She tripped over a root and plopped to her knees. Alec sent all the loose pinecones flying as he jumped forward to scoop her out of the snow. She looked at him in surprise, as if wondering how he'd gotten there so fast.

"Falldown," she said matter-of-factly, wiping more dirt and snow on her snowsuit than she'd needed to brush off.

He kissed her forehead, the only clean spot on her, and set her back down. "Mama's waiting for us. We better get back."

She said something he didn't understand and darted in the direction of the cabin. He followed her slowly, smiling a little, more at peace at that moment than at any other in his life.

That peculiar sensation of being watched stole over him and he stopped to look up at the cabin's narrow veranda. Cait stood outside, his old serape draped around her shoulders like a poncho. Her face was flushed from cooking their Thanksgiving Day dinner and her hair stuck up in those spiky points he found so endlessly fascinating.

She caught Allie as she flew up the steps and held her tightly as she smiled down the hill at him. She looked down at something Allie said, chuckled a little, and removed Allie's hood and ruffled her dark curls. Then she pointed down where Alec stood watching them.

Allie's face lit up as if she hadn't seen him in hours. Her blue eyes sparkled, her toothy grin flashed.

"Daddy!" she called. "Daddy!"

Alec's heart constricted painfully. Wonderfully.

Cait blew him a kiss and held her hand up in greeting. Her wedding ring caught a stray beam of sunlight and glittered on her hand. He felt as if he couldn't breathe, that if he moved a single muscle this beautiful, incredible fantasy would slip away and he wouldn't know how to go to sleep deeply enough to dream it back again.

Cait started chuckling. "Did you leave any pinecones in the forest?" She pointed at his bulging pockets.

He stuck in his hand to pull one free and pricked his finger on a sharp point. Running the rest of the way to the veranda, he gathered Cait and Allie in his arms and held them tight, pressing his cheeks to theirs.

"It wasn't a dream," he declared. "You're really here."

Cait lifted her warm hand to his ice-cold face. "Always," she said. "Some dreams do come true."

* * * * *

The exciting new cross-line continuity series about love, marriage—and Daddy's unexpected need for a baby carriage!

🥕🥕🥕🥕🥕🥕🥕

You loved

THE BABY NOTION by Dixie Browning (Desire #1011 7/96)
and
BABY IN A BASKET by Helen R. Myers
(Romance #1169 8/96)

Now the series continues with...

MARRIED...WITH TWINS! by Jennifer Mikels
(Special Edition #1054 9/96)

The soon-to-be separated Kincaids just found out they're about to be parents. Will their newfound family grant them a second chance at marriage?

Don't miss the next books in this wonderful series:

HOW TO HOOK A HUSBAND (AND A BABY)
by Carolyn Zane (Yours Truly #29 10/96)

DISCOVERED: DADDY
by Marilyn Pappano (Intimate Moments #746 11/96)

DADDY KNOWS LAST continues each month...
only from

Silhouette®
TM

Bestselling Author

MERLINE
LOVELACE

Continues the twelve-book series—FORTUNE'S CHILDREN
in September 1996 with Book Three

BEAUTY AND THE BODYGUARD

Ex-mercenary Rafe Stone was Fortune Cosmetics cover girl
Allie Fortune's best protection against an obsessed stalker. He
was also the one man this tempting beauty was willing to risk
her heart for....

MEET THE FORTUNES—a family whose legacy is greater than
riches. Because where there's a will...there's a *wedding!*

A CASTING CALL TO
ALL FORTUNE'S CHILDREN FANS!
If you are truly one of the fortunate
few, you may win a trip to
Los Angeles to audition for
Wheel of Fortune®. Look for
details in all retail Fortune's Children titles!

Look us up on-line at: http://www.romance.net

FC-3-C-R

Your very favorite Silhouette miniseries characters now have a BRAND-NEW story in

Brought to you by:

LINDA HOWARD

DEBBIE MACOMBER

LINDA TURNER

LINDA HOWARD celebrates the holidays with a **Mackenzie** wedding—once Maris regains her memory, that is....

DEBBIE MACOMBER brings **Those Manning Men** and **The Manning Sisters** home for a mistletoe marriage as a single dad finally says "I do."

LINDA TURNER brings **The Wild West** alive as Priscilla Rawlings ties the knot at the Double R Ranch.

Three BRAND-NEW holiday love stories...by romance fiction's most beloved authors.

Available in November at your favorite retail outlet.

Silhouette®

As seen on TV!

Free Gift Offer

With a Free Gift proof-of-purchase from any Silhouette® book,
you can receive a beautiful cubic zirconia pendant.

This gorgeous marquise-shaped stone is a genuine cubic
zirconia—accented by an 18" gold tone necklace.

(Approximate retail value $19.95)

Send for yours today...

compliments of ▼ *Silhouette*®
™

To receive your free gift, a cubic zirconia pendant, send us one original proof-of-
purchase, photocopies not accepted, from the back of any Silhouette Romance™,
Silhouette Desire®, Silhouette Special Edition®, Silhouette Intimate Moments®
or Silhouette Yours Truly™ title available in August, September or October at your favorite
retail outlet, together with the Free Gift Certificate, plus a check or money order for
$1.65 U.S./$2.15 CAN. (do not send cash) to cover postage and handling, payable
to Silhouette Free Gift Offer. We will send you the specified gift. Allow 6 to 8 weeks for
delivery. Offer good until October 31, 1996 or while quantities last. Offer valid in the
U.S. and Canada only.

Free Gift Certificate

Name: _____

Address: _____

City: _____ State/Province: _____ Zip/Postal Code: _____

Mail this certificate, one proof-of-purchase and a check or money order for postage
and handling to: SILHOUETTE FREE GIFT OFFER 1996. In the U.S.: 3010 Walden
Avenue, P.O. Box 9077, Buffalo NY 14269-9077. In Canada: P.O. Box 613, Fort Erie,
Ontario L2Z 5X3.

FREE GIFT OFFER   084-KMD

ONE PROOF-OF-PURCHASE

To collect your fabulous FREE GIFT, a cubic zirconia pendant, you must include this
original proof-of-purchase for each gift with the properly completed Free Gift Certificate.

084-KMD

There's nothing quite like a family

REUNION

HANNAH · MICHAEL · KATE

The new miniseries by
Pat Warren

Three siblings are about to be reunited.
And each finds love along the way....

HANNAH
Her life is about to change now that she's met
the irresistible Joel Merrick in HOME FOR HANNAH
(Special Edition #1048, August 1996).

MICHAEL
He's been on his own all his life. Now he's
going to take a risk on love...and
take part in the reunion he's been
waiting for in MICHAEL'S HOUSE
(Intimate Moments #737, September 1996).

KATE
A job as a nanny leads her to Aaron Carver,
his adorable baby daughter and the
fulfillment of her dreams in KEEPING KATE
(Special Edition #1060, October 1996).

Meet these three siblings from

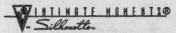

Silhouette SPECIAL EDITION®
and

INTIMATE MOMENTS®
Silhouette

Look us up on-line at: http://www.romance.net

REUNION

You're About to Become a
Privileged Woman

Reap the rewards of fabulous free gifts and benefits with proofs-of-purchase from Silhouette and Harlequin books

Pages & Privileges™

It's our way of thanking you for buying our books at your favorite retail stores.

```
┌─────────────────────────────┐
│  PROOF OF      SIM-PP171     │
│  PURCHASE                    │
│ Offer expires October 31,1996│
└─────────────────────────────┘
```

Harlequin and Silhouette— the most privileged readers in the world!

For more information about Harlequin and Silhouette's PAGES & PRIVILEGES program call the Pages & Privileges Benefits Desk: 1-503-794-2499

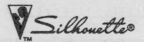

SIM-PP171